Two Too Good
Two Is Always Better Than One

By K.K Cambric

Copyright © 2024 K.K Cambric
All rights reserved.
ISBNs: 979-8-89324-142-6

Printed in the United States of America.

No part of this publication shall be reproduced, transmitted, or sold in whole or in part in any form without the prior written consent of the author, except as provided by the United States of America copyright law. Any unauthorized usage of the text without express written permission of the publisher is a violation of the author's copyright and is illegal and punishable by law. All trademarks and registered trademarks appearing in this guide are the property of their respective owners.

The opinions expressed by the Author are not necessarily those held by the publisher.

The information contained within this book is strictly for informational purposes. The material may include information, products, or services by third parties. As such, the Author and Publisher do not assume responsibility or liability for any third-party material or opinions. The publisher is not responsible for websites (or their content) that are not owned by the publisher. Readers are advised to do their own due diligence when it comes to making decisions.

I dedicate this Book to my Mother, Yvette M Jackson. Mom, I wouldn't have done this any other way, as you would say, why not? I'm sorry, Ms. Jackson, whew, this book is for real. My forever Angel, Rest In Paradise. I did it, MOM!

Contents

Acknowledgments

Chapter 1 - Him...1

Chapter 2 - Surprised...5

Chapter 3 - Confused..10

Chapter 4 - What the Fuck?..13

Chapter 5 - Adeventure AM..18

Chapter 6 - Business mixed with Pleasure..24

Chapter 7 - Thirsty Thursday..31

Chapter 8 - Michael Washington..37

Chapter 9 - Funky Attitude...41

Chapter 10 - Friday night...45

Chapter 11 - Controversy Bullshit...53

Chapter 12 - Damage Control..59

Chapter 13 - MotorMouth Sundaze..66

Chapter 14 - Truthful Monday...73

Chapter 15 - Discussions & Decisions...79

About the Author..85

Acknowledgments

I first want to say thank you, God, for giving me the strength, discipline, and creative mind to write.

I want to say thank you to my friend Erick M. Moore for helping me design my vision for the cover of my book. Your Talent didn't go unnoticed or unappreciated.

I want to say thank You to my Pops, Antyreon E. Cambric, for spending nights on the phone with me, giving me ideas on my visions, and helping proofread certain things. I am very grateful.

Thank you to my friends who truly encouraged me to do this. You all know who you are. My kids allowed me space to write.

Chapter 1
Him

It was a gloomy, stormy Wednesday. I was at work looking at the clock like I was ready to go in my mind. I was like, will I call him or pull out my toy and have a great time with the bottle of sweet Marcella? Oh, how that drink with a splash of Cîroc pineapple makes me do amazing things. In the meantime, while I was finishing up at work and logging off my computer, I received a text message.

"Hey sexy, are you free tonight?" I thought to myself, *right on time*. Of course, I didn't respond right away. You know, I can't show my excitement so quickly because then it will show sprung. I laughed out loud. As I walked out of the office, I got a phone call, and it was from him. I guess he couldn't wait for a response. The excitement on my face and my voice; I couldn't wait to see him tonight. The way that man touches my body makes me cum woo! Oh, the chemistry we share! The bedroom is fucking amazing. Too bad he's not boyfriend material; we fuck all the time. I cut short our conversation. I want to leave his imagination, what I will do to him tonight.

As we hung up the phone, my kitty was purring for great sex. I was excited about fucking him tonight. Then I let out a great sigh, "Ahhhh, how I'll hold his dick in my hands with my stones shining and *blinging* in the light; my nail tech was a beast and outdid herself this time. My nail tech could never. As I slowly teased his head, I sucked on him with my natural plump lips wrapped around his beautiful chocolate dick, wrapping it around with my tongue, giving him soft slurps and caressing his dick with so much enthusiasm."

Now that I was all excited about pleasing him, I needed to get myself together as I got home. I fixed myself some dinner and tidied up the house. Ha, why when we get a man coming over, we clean up extra tidily? I laughed out loud. A house can be a wreck all week, but when he calls, the house gets spot-clean, ha-ha. Woo, wine is on, and chill music is going. I hopped in the shower real quick and caressed my perky pierced breast, just thinking about how he sucks on them and stares me in my eyes and fucks me with such good thrust. I feel every inch of him as I continue to wash my triple-D breasts. I took my washcloth with extra soapy water and washed my thick thighs that wrapped around his neck as my legs rested behind his head. Oh my God, I have myself so worked up already to fuck the shit out of this gorgeous chocolate-bearded man.

Then I got out of this amazing steamy shower, all horny and ready for my fun of interest for the night, encountered with great sex, laughter, and conversations. That man's pillow talk is so different. A woman can only dream that his heart would only open up for love, not just any love but pure, unconditional love. A lady can dream just like how Cinderella had a prince. What the fucking glass slipper. Why can't my ass dream? Anywho, whatever, I need to caress my body with some oils and smell good. He loves and appreciates how good I taste and smell. I think it's very important because these heffas are out here, stinking. Woo, chill, help them lord!

I put on my short booty shorts and see-through tank top, showing off my 40 triple DD perky pierced nipples and my natural big booty Judy cheeks that peekaboo out of my shorts. I poured myself a chilled, hefty glass of sweet Marcella with a shot of pineapple Cîroc. It was definitely a crazy ass day at work; being a senior VP at an exclusive about to be a Fortune 500 company has been crazy and stressful, so me Getting fucked tonight is a release this cutie needs, OK. My phone rings. It's him.

He said, "Hello, sexy. I'm leaving work. Are you ready to have an amazing night with me?" As I tried not to get all excited, I said, "Yes, I'm sure I am. What time shall I expect you?" He said, "Sexy, I shall be there by 11 PM at his request. Make sure you have on those sexy shorts I like when I get there." I responded, "Yes, honey, got it covered! And then we hung up. I was all smiles. It's sick how much this man makes me blush. I hate it, but I love it all at the same time.

As I was sipping on my wine, someone came knocking at the door. I hesitated as I wasn't expecting anyone. Then I heard three more knocks. I'm like, who the fuck is at my door at 10:03 PM? Let me check my camera, trying to be quiet because people who know me know that I don't do pop-ups. I'll leave y'all's ass straight outside. Rain, sleet, snow, African hot, ha-ha. Anyway, I proceeded to the door; it was just my bugaboo neighbor asking if my lights were flaring through the house, etc. I'm like, "Hey girlfriend, yes, they are. Is this some power outage or something going on?" I asked. She said, "Who knows!" I cut her short and said, "Well, it's late. Keep me posted. I'm going to call it a night." I could tell she wanted to keep talking. As mom used to say while laughing, "Bye, chatty Kathy, honey."

I couldn't let her keep talking. All I could focus on was a sexy chocolate man with a good dick on the way. As I proceeded to walk back to the living room and enjoy my glass of wine, my phone kept ringing. I was like, what the fuck is with tonight? Hell, my phone hasn't had this much jumping since I was outside in the streets like the *Lady in the Tramp days*, hahaha. Then I proceeded to look at my caller ID to see who it was; it said 'private.' I can only imagine who that might be. Ahh, no, sir, that ship has sailed into the harbor and drowned. Who the hell does he think he is? Still thinking about his access to me and my tight juicy pussy, man, please, or should I say Negro, please. But why when I gave the call the fuck you button, the caller has the nerve to call right back, not once but twice! I was like, damn, at this point could it be an emergency? So my dumbass answered with sarcasm.

"Hello," I heard crickets. As I was about to hang up, I heard, "Wait, baby! I love you, my queen. I know I fucked up. Just let me... Let me see you. Let me explain."

My heart dropped into my stomach like, what the fuck? I've been waiting on those words for years, but all I can think about was my night of great passion, hot and heated sex with Mr. Pillow talker, Mr. Pleaser. Why did I have to answer this call right now at 10:30 PM on a Wednesday night? I'm frozen like a bag of peas. All I heard was, "Baby sweetheart, my Nubian queen, are you there?" I couldn't believe this was happening. A bitch was speechless. I was like, "Yes, I'm here, but now wasn't a good time. Let's talk tomorrow!" He wasn't hearing me. He was like let me come over, or you can come here, please all I could think about was *him* on his way to fulfill all my needs right at this given time. My mind was like, why now? Why tonight, when I was about to be fed some good dick and scrumptious eye candy with that thick-ass beard and the muscles squeezing me as we enjoy every amazing fuck session, sometimes 2-3 times a night. Fuck, he was really on my phone; Michael Washington ass, who I had for many years, who

I loved for many years, who broke my heart, and took years to move on, but he chose his career instead of me.

I had to answer him quickly before he got here. I can't lie; this kind of fucked up my mood like what the fuck. I was trying to quickly make a decision. Do I cancel him and see who I've always wanted, or do I wait and see Michael during my time? What the hell do I do? I kept thinking in my mind, come on girl, haha, so I said, "Well, Michael, no, I won't see you tonight. I haven't heard from you in years, and you can't just come back into my life and think I'm gonna just drop shit to meet up and please you. I know I will call you when I'm ready to see you and go from there. Have an amazing night. Good night!" I hung up the phone before he could get a word in. Who does that man think he is? Nope, why am I still wrecking my mind? Like, did this man really just call me like really God? My prayers are getting mixed up. I was laughing really hard at that moment, ha ha ha...

Chapter 2
Surprise

My phone was ringing again. I was like, oh my God, what or who, now? It's him. As I was unlocking the door, he said, "Hey sexy, I'm outside. I am here, and I can't wait to kiss both of your lips." I was like, "OK honey, see you in a few. My mood has totally changed, but glad he's here to take my mind off the shit that just happened. I'm like, let me sit this wine down and try to calm myself down so I can enjoy and devour this sexy, dark chocolate man that I've been craving all night.

Knock knock, I'm like, babe, stop playing. You just called me and told me to unlock the door. Come get me. I'm definitely looking forward to kissing those sexy, big juicy lips and those tight hugs you give me, squeezing my ass with those big strong hands. Ugh, I am still hearing knocking at the damn door. I'm like, who the fuck is knocking? I don't have my phone to check the camera, so I'm like, okay, let me just open the door with all this sexiness. He just wants to play with me tonight; okay, I kinda like it cause I was walking towards the door. My phone was ringing, but I kept ignoring it because my sexy *chocolate* was here, and I was just focused on him and our night.

I opened the door to find out who was standing there. Looking good, yes, good as fuck was Mr. Fucking Michael Washington! Oh my God, my eyes were big as hell. The only thing I could do was just stand there frozen. Oh my God, oh my God, what the fuck I'm gonna do...

"Hey babe, why do you look so surprised to see me?" Like, for real? I'm thinking, what the fuck is this fine-ass man doing at my doorstep when I clearly told him I would call him when I'm ready? I thought while shaking my damn head.

"Hello, KaiAndra, what is the problem?"

"Michael, really, why are you here? I thought I just told you I would call you when I'm ready, but tonight is not the night. Why the fuck do you think the world revolves around your ass? This is another reason why we have problems or don't work out."

All I could think about was what the fuck was I going to do... What the fuck was I going to do? Explain to *him* why I had another man standing in front of my door at almost 11-ish p.m. on a Wednesday night. I laughed out loud.

The door slammed from the parking garage, and I heard footsteps. Oh my God, he is coming. Think bitch! Think! All of a sudden, I heard, "Hey baby, you are looking fine as hell, and I can't wait to taste that juicy pussy." Oh my God, here we go, the man that I used to fuck consistently fell in love with me all over again. Just heard my no-strings-attached good- head-giving-sucking-toes-man come for me; shit, fuck, fire!! All I could do was stand there, looking crazy.

I heard, "Babe, why are you outside in the hallway looking good as fuck, and who is this man?"

I said, "Hey, babe!" Before I could say anything else, Michael said, "I was coming to see an old friend, but clearly, I have the wrong apartment. I must have forgotten her building. My apologies, y'all. It looks like y'all gonna have a fun night. Sorry for interrupting y'all. Have a good night."

Wow, I thought to myself, this man was about to bust my ass in front of my company. Now, he's definitely up to something. The old Mr. Washington would never be like that.

"Oh, no problem. You have an amazing night!" He said as he picked me up, carried me inside my apartment, and laid me down on the couch. All I could think about was Michael's fine ass. I can't believe he showed up like that in the middle of the night. What the fuck? He thought he was gonna get some of this coochie tonight, wow!

Finally, I was somewhat distracted by *him* kissing my inner thighs and massaging my body. I was starting to get in the mood again. My pussy was starting to beat really fast. I was very horny. I'd been wanting him all night. He opened my legs, and he kissed the inside of my thighs, making his way up to my pussy. I was moaning with his tongue and lips, giving me pleasure. He was teasing my *lips* and giving them soft kisses as his tongue stroked my clit. Woo! This man knows my body, I thought. He made my body sing as I caressed his fresh bald head deeper into my pussy. I was about to cum; I moaned;

"Yes, fuck! Fuck! She's about to cum baby." He was into it as well. "Cum for me, baby," he said.

Oh my God! I was so into him, but I had to stay focused and remember that KaiAndra, you cannot catch feelings for this man; he isn't relationship material, just fuck- worthy. Yeah, I did just make that up and laughed out loud.

He said, "Baby, you want some of this chocolate bar?"

I told him that I wanted to taste him first, and I wanted to return the pleasure and please him before we fuck. I kissed him, and I loved that he didn't get all weirded out. I mean, it was my pussy that I tasted anyways, but it's the same when I'll give him head.

I took his hand and led him to my bedroom. I have an amazing bedroom, 850 ft.^{2} walking closet, and a master bedroom with a balcony. As we lay on the bed, I kissed his hips and made my way to his pretty 8-inch sexy chocolate dick. I mean, I had never seen a dick so pretty. I wrapped my long, stiletto-blinged-out nails, and I began to slurp on the tip and tease its head with my tongue and soft kisses against the shaft. All I could hear was, "Fuck, fuck, fuck, KaiAndra! Why are you sucking my dick like this? You're gonna make a man fall deeper in love with you with no regrets!"

I said, "It's just the tongue, baby. You know you don't want a relationship for the things that come with it." He tried, though. He said, "KaiAndra, you're gonna make me cum, and I want some of that tight juicy ass pussy to cum all over me," as I pulled his sexy chocolate dick from my lips. I kissed my way up to the top. I climbed up on his ass and guided him into my wet pussy. I was so tight; a lady hasn't had none in forever. I mean, I don't sleep around. I take care of my pocketbook. I ain't a hoe! I mean, maybe I do have some tendencies with my mate, but that's about it. Ha ha ha, I liked it.

He was like, "Fuck! Fuck, wait, don't move, babe. Hold on! "He was telling me to wait. Why though, I know he ain't about to cum. I just know he's not. Then I heard, "OK, babe! Sorry, you are so tight. I had to get comfortable and not cum so fast." Then he continued in his Johnny Gill voice, "Your pussy! My My My! You love me, don't you?"

Oh my God, why would he ask me this in the middle of an amazing session we were in? I can't say the wrong thing because then our session will be over, ha ha. I still want him to hit me from the back or missionary. I had to lock eyes with this man. I do love him, but I know deep down in my heart he couldn't have loved me like I needed and wanted.

"Babe! Did you not hear me?" Fuck, why he always got a fuck up a good thing.

"Yes, babe, I love you. I love this dick, too, but let's not talk about this right now. Fuck, fuck! Imma cum. She's about to cum all over him, babe." He said, "Yes, baby. Yes, give me, give me you, cum all over him."

As I started to slow down, he flipped my thick ass over, pulled me towards the end of the bed, and whispered, "This is my pussy. Don't get fucked up, KaiAndra. I love you, woman. I know you think I'm not ready to be the man you need, and I have mommy issues, but what you don't know is what I've seen... I've been seeing a therapist and doing a lot more self-care for myself. God dammit this pussy is so good! I'm ready to fully commit to us, babe," as I was about to cum again. I was enjoying this man. I brushed off his bullshit conversation. He always talks this bullshit during our sessions because our chemistry is the bomb. Honestly, the shit it's so amazing.

I laughed and said, "You're about to cum with me, babe, aren't you?" As I wiped the sweat from his face and kissed him passionately.

"Of course, he says, KaiAndra, listen, I want you full-time all the time. You're an amazing businesswoman, loving, kind, funny, and with a great personality. I'd be a dummy to let you slip away... I'm about to cum. Oh shit, get your pussy babe. Get your pussy! Fuck, Fuck!" As we both came together. It was so needed, and I loved every minute and second of his chocolate dick.

He pulled out of me, and I always loved to taste him, but he literally ran from me. He made a smart-ass comment as he was pushing me away from trying not to suck his dick. He said, "I know that it was Michael Washington at your front door this evening." I tried not to give him a reaction, but in my mind, I was like, how in the fuck does he know about Michael Washington.

Chapter 3
Confused

All I can say was nothing, speechless as fuck. He told me not to lie to him. I knew that was him, didn't I? As I was silent. I was like, what the fuck? Why do I keep getting put in these awkward positions with these two men?

"Well, babe, if you know so much, you should know the answer, right?"

"KaiAndra, don't fucking play with me?"

"Umm, excuse me, don't get loud, and you're not my man. I don't owe you an explanation or anything. I can remember a time you told me when I asked you who you were with over a weekend or who you went on a trip with. You told me, "Don't worry about it. It doesn't concern you." Oops, did you forget that conversation?"

"Here you go. You took that wrong, and you ran with it." "Whatever, you almost fucked up that night being an asshole."

"KaiAndra, answer the fucking question, woman! Was it Michael Washington?"

"Yes, babe, it was." His reaction was different. I didn't know he knew, but I didn't know he cared. The fuck is going on right now.

"Why? Why, like, why do you even care? We just fucked from time to time. You fell off hard. We don't even go on dates or hang out past these four walls or outside my California king-sized bed, so what's all the questions for?"

"KaiAndra? It may seem like I'm a dick, as you say, or an asshole but babe, I want you. I want us to have a future, go on vacations, laugh, continue our great sessions, etc... I love you, woman. You are for me, and I'm working on myself every day to be a better man for myself, my kids, and for us."

Oh my God, what is tonight? Usher night, these are my confessions, fuck. All I could think about now was how good this man just fucked me and made me cum like Niagra Falls like that. I laughed out loud, and oh, how this man sexy ass hell.

My God, I couldn't believe Michael Washington just showed up at my door after all these years and played it cool like it wasn't shit. I was with another man. He says ahh, hello, I hear you babe. I'm thinking to myself, why the change? I'm supposed to believe you had an epiphany, and now you want me. Yeah, right, I think you just saw that man who you knew I was with for years and was like, oh hell no, he ain't about to get what's been mine for some years, that's what the fuck I thought.

"Well, it's 3 AM. I gotta get some sleep. Are you gonna get dressed and go home? You know, you don't stay the night anymore; remember, you always have stuff to do blah blah blah whomp whomp, I'll walk you out."

"KaiAndra"

"Oh yeah, that's my name. You called it very well tonight." I laughed out loud. "I must have done my job. Stop it! "

"Stop what?" he says.

"OK, we can continue this over dinner this weekend if you're free," I began to answer.

He interrupted me and said, "I will not take no for an answer."

"Well, OK, pick me up at eight. I'll be ready now to go home so I can get some sleep. I have a meeting at 9 AM. I am tired."

There was a lot that happened tonight. I was still in shock as I was putting on my shorts and tank. He was fully dressed, still smelling good as fuck. I walked him to the front door and kissed him passionately as I was gonna miss him. And that man can kiss! Lord have mercy.

I pulled away and said, "OK, babe, before we end up back in my bed fucking again, I opened the front door, and standing there was this man who was fine, tall, caramel, clean, cut, fresh, cut, smelling good, gorgeous smile Mr. Fucking Michael Washington back at my door, my fucking door at 3 AM. I knew it. I knew he went away too quickly.

Chapter 4
What the Fuck?

Why, oh my God, why is this happening to me again? Babe knows who this man is. This can't be good. What in the entire fuck am I gonna do now shit!!! This can't be happening. Two fine-ass men, one I enjoy fucking and one that I was in love with for years. What in the entire fuck am I gonna do now? Shit!

So as we are all standing at my door at 3:05 a.m. in the fucking morning, this sexy ass *caramelicious* man says hey KaiAndra, I couldn't just get your fine ass off my mind like I let you get away once, but I'll be damned if I let your gorgeous self get away twice.

"I see you had your fun for the night. Your company is leaving, and now you have time to talk."

Who the fuck does this man think he is? Like honestly, I'm flattered, but oh my God, I just cannot do this to him. I'm still speechless at this point, but all of a sudden, I heard, "Hey, man. I'm Malachi, KaiAndra's no-strings fuck-buddy; nice to meet you, Michael Washington! That is your name, correct? KaiAndra's ex from some years ago?" Me. I'm still speechless.

"Hello Malachi, yes, I'm an executive CO of Karmi Sports. I am sure you've heard of the business. Nice to meet you. I'm sure y'all had an eventful night. Sorry for interrupting. Looks like you were just leaving. That was a quick night, I see."

"Michael! Stop it." I said. I was so embarrassed at this point. What the fuck is this man thinking about right now.

"Well, for your information, we had an amazing night, and I would have loved to stay, but the lady needs her rest, and if I had stayed, she wouldn't make it for her meeting in the morning because I am that guy."

Chuckles came from Michael as he said, "OK, dude, whatever you say.

Well, aren't you leaving? No strings, oh my bad Malachi."

I chimed in. "Yes, he was leaving. And he was right. I have a big meeting at 9 AM with some big executives, and I'm pretty tired."

I believe I said we would talk tomorrow and figure out what day works best for me, as I was interrupted by Malachi babe, "I'm going to go. I see you have a fan club and shit, so I will call you after your meeting and go from there. Good night, babe."

"OK, babe, good night. Tonight was great. Be safe and dream about me."

Yes, I went there. I know Michael has plenty of bitches, so whatever. I heard, "Michael, are you done? So can I come in and talk about us?"

Is this man for real, like he ain't taking no for an answer?

"Michael, KaiAndra, stop the bullshit and let me come in. I see you already got fucked tonight, so it ain't like I'm a go behind that man. Nope, I want My own session on my time; definitely won't be no-strings-attached fucking with me. KaiAndra, what the fuck? When did you start this shit?"

"Come again, Start what shit, Michael?" "Friends with benefits?"

"Really? Why the questions? Why do you care anyway? Michael fuck you. You were my everything, my best friend, my lover, my shoulder, my partner, and you just left. What, Michael, why are you looking confused?"

"Can I come the fuck in? Damn! Got me out in this hallway,"

"Fine shit, it's not like you're gonna leave anyway. What the fuck do you want, Michael? What is it? Why can't it wait until tomorrow?"

"KaiAndra" "What, Michael, why you gotta say my name like that? It's almost 4 AM. What do you want? Why are you so angry, Michael? It's 4 AM. I just had a great night with an amazing man, and now you're at my house again unannounced yet again, and it's almost 4 AM, and you won't tell me what you want, so hello, what is it that you want?"

"KaiAndra" third time.

"You keep saying my name and still ain't said what you want from me?"

"Babe, I don't want anything but your love, your heart, your body, your soul. KaiAndra, please just listen, baby; you are my queen, and I should have chosen you in my career. I'm sorry my head got big. I got picked up by a big investor out of Kansas City, and he gave me over 1 million and start-up money, and I had to rush on it. I'm sorry I didn't know how to involve you in my career. These last three years have been amazing but not as amazing as if it would have been with you and doing it with you. I think about you. I dream about you. I cannot get you out of my mind. You are my soulmate. You are why my business has succeeded. It was all because of you, babe."

As I was sitting here listening to this sappy bullshit, he's trying to feed me, rolling my eyes and looking at my oven clock saying 4:25 AM, I heard, "KaiAndra, are you listening to me?"

"Michael, I hear you. Do I believe you now? Nope, absolutely bullshit to me. You saw a Brutha at my door earlier, and what you left and made up some bullshit that I just fell to my knees and believe you yeah OK the fuck I don't think so like miss me with the sentimental bullshit Michael I've seen all the social media shit you and your chocolate bitch you got parading all over the Internet for years so stop it you had time for her ass and then some so don't come back over here trying to make nice cause y'all didn't Work. Fuck you and your story Michael. Really, why are you here? What do you want? I just got fucked really good tonight, and you're killing my vibe."

"Oh, so you're into bald-headed negroes now, huh?"

"I sure am. Fine, thick, tall, chocolate ones, too. Why are you so concerned?"

"KaiAndra!"

"Negro! If you call my name one more time."

"What is it, woman? I fucked up. OK, I made a rational decision and ran off. I'm sorry I texted and called you, but you blocked me. Why?"

"Because you hurt me, dummy. I gave you five years and a miscarriage. You promised me after college, we were gonna be forever and put a lockdown on our future. You left me. That's some weak shit to do to someone you love. I really think you should leave. I need my rest. I have an important meeting in the morning."

He said, "Fine. But this isn't over. I'mma get my woman back at every cost, and trust me, that Malachi guy, whatever his name is, will not be your no-strings-attached for what I gotta say about it."

"Ha, if you say so, why the fuck do you care so much? He has been fucking and sucking on my pussy for years."

"That's my point. That's all he has to offer you. That man knows you taste good and feel good and that you are a good woman who respects her body. Shit! Who wouldn't? I would love to have another chance and do the right thing for you. I'm a go, but I just know I am not a man who gives up easily. I will be awaiting your call, but don't take long because I will pop up again. Don't play with me.

As I rolled my eyes, I was like, "Whatever, Michael, don't think you could just come back into my life, and everything can go back to us, not no fucking way you lost your fucking mind. I'm going to bed for the third time. Good night, Michael, damn!"

"Good night, babe," I said as I was walking his fine ass to the door and my phone rang. I'm like, here we go. I turn around, and it's him, Malachi.

"Hey babe, I just wanted to call you to make sure you're OK. I made it safe."

"Well, this is new. You haven't done this in years." I thought to myself; What are these men on big bullshit tonight?

"Yes, babe, when we were fucking I meant every got damn word I said to you?

"Oh, is that right? OK, well, that's... let's talk more about it tomorrow or, better yet, Saturday night, or was that just bullshit because that head I gave you was fire" I laughed out loud. "Good night, Malachi."

"Good night, my baby. I love you."

"Yeah, love you too." As I hung up the phone, I didn't realize Michael was still in the doorway.

"Oh, so you love this cornball. Really, KaiAndra? A guy you have no strings attached to, and you love him. yeah?"

OK, damn, was this fool really listening to my conversation? "Michael, as I don't owe you an explanation, yes, I love him, Malachi. Yes, it's more than just sex for me anyway. I don't have to explain shit to your ass. Good night, leave, and be safe. Goodbye.

"Well, for what it's worth, KaiAndra. I never stopped loving you, and I will show you no matter how long it takes to prove it."

Chapter 5
Adventure AM

"Yeah, I've heard all this bullshit before. The fuck! Do I look like boo-boo the fool? Bye, Michael, I'll call you."

"OK, babe."

What a night! A bitch got fed a good dick, and two men said they wanted me. The hell, this is crazy, but what the fuck in the same sentence? I have to lie down and get some sleep these few hours. I wonder what kind of dreams I'mma have tonight. Whew, good night, fuck.

As this weak-ass alarm goes off at 7 AM, I just had to stop and think, what the fuck just happened last night? Like I'm still saying, what the fuck, chile?

Good morning, As I get my fine ass up and ready for a shower, my doorbell goes off. I grab my phone like, *who in the hell is that at my mother fucking door at 7 AM?* **Damn**, you won't believe this shit... it's him. Malachi, this man never comes over to my house unannounced or comes to my house this early. What the fuck, more shenanigans? He rings my bell again. "OK, OK, I'm coming. Damn," I open the door. This man looks so good and smells so good. "Hey." I continued, "Hey, what are you..." Before I could get the rest out, he passionately kisses me, picks me up, shuts the door behind us, and carries me into the bedroom. I'm like, "OK, good morning. I'm happy to see you too, but what do I owe this unannounced visit for?"

As he's about to answer, my breasts popped out of my robe, just as perky as fuck. Looking at him, snapping my fingers as I said, "Helm, Malachi," as he was staring at my 40 triple D pierced perky breast.

"Babe, I woke up with you in my mind, and I needed to feel you and taste you before you got your day started. I'm sorry, I normally don't do this shit, but when you turn me on, my dick is so hard, it's crazy sometimes. Are you mad?"

In my mind, morning wood, breakfast dick, hell yes, mad no, but my meeting is at 9 AM. Oh my God, sex before work, fuck, KaiAndra.

"Yes, babe, where did you go?" "Sorry, yes, babe, fuck me."

We don't have much time as I still need to shower. I find myself removing this man's clothes, and his dick is ready to fuck. He picks me up and puts me against the wall, and I came down on his dick so smoothly. We both moaned, ummm, and said fuck as he sucked on my left breast with such force he made me cum, and I feel his thrusting in and out of me, him getting faster and faster as I felt he was about to come.

I'm about to scream; this man feels so good. "God dammit, she's so wet and juicy. Oh my God," I yell out, "yes, babe, fuck me harder. Fuck me now, this is your pussy, get it."

He walks over to the bed. "Fuck me some more." He pushes my legs behind my head and fucks me some more while our eyes are locked, and he says, "Kai, I love you, and I'm ready to be that man for you," and pulls out as we came together. Ain't nothing like morning sex with a sexy mate.

As I was about to get up, he said, "Hold on, babe. Let me taste you." I was like, "Babe, you know I got a meeting. I still need to shower at 7:35 AM, and you know about Tallahassee's traffic."

"I got you, just lay back and relax. Oh my God!" I could get used to this, but I feel like he, Malachi, is just showing off because he saw Michael last night. Oh my God, this man's lips are so soft against my lips. He's gonna make me scream.

I came two more times; this man, this man, he could be my man. Fuck, what about Michael? Fuck it, I'm enjoying the moment as I say, "Thank you, babe, for the surprise dick and amazing head. I got to get in the shower," he said, "Okay, let's get in the shower," as he proceeded to the bathroom to join me.

My phone rings. It's one of the executives calling. I'm like, "Fuck, I'm all hot and disturbed. Let me get my shit together."

"KaiAndra Barnes speaking,"

"Hey, KaiAndra, this is Jax. We have to move the meeting to 11 AM. Is that gonna work for you?"

"Oh, absolutely. I have nothing on my agenda until 3 PM today." "Great, glad I could catch you before rolling through Tallahassee

traffic."

"Yes, thanks. We'll look at that, more time to play before work," as I walk into the bathroom. This man has my water running with his fine ass in it. Woo, he is so fine. Damn, he's my weakness, chocolate, bald, and that beard.

I stepped into my shower; he kissed me so passionately. My breasts immediately get hard; this man turns me on so expeditiously. I just can't help it, fuck, as I pull away from him. I get on my knees and pull him close to me as I devour his dick in my mouth softly, gently, from his shaft to his head. I teased him, kissed his balls, and caressed them all at the same time. I hear him moaning as it's turning me on too. All I hear is, "fuck, Kai, fuck, you just doing ya thang, fuck."

As I'm sucking his dick, it's getting harder. I slowly remove my mouth and sit him down on my shower stoop and straddle him while I spread my legs and guide him inside of me. I start fucking him slowly, back and forth at first. I love riding him. His dick fits my body perfectly. He pulls my breast to his lips, sucking on them like an orange or watermelon. As we are both moaning, "Ugh, oooh yes, fuck me," he's saying, "Yes babe, fuck me, cum on me."

As I'm riding, I'm getting faster and faster. I feel we are about to cum together. He's still sucking my pierced nipples as I'm still cumming. As my body is shivering, he grabs my washcloth with my Dove body wash and washes my body from the top of my chest to my arms, my stomach, my thighs, legs, ass, and feet.

Oh my God, what is this man doing to me? Why is he loving me like this? Did Michael become a threat? I'm so confused. "Malachi, what is this all about, babe? We've been fucking for years; you never showed up at my house for breakfast sex, what's up, babe?"

"I don't know, babe. Now," "But what-"

"Let me finish."

"God, I know how much of a real woman you are. I know we started off rocky and crazy. We both were shitty to each other, and I know you want more time, and I just didn't give it to you, so basically, you said fuck me and buried your ass into your company and fucked with me occasionally. I understand that now."

"Malachi, don't kill the vibe with that weak-ass bullshit story; you know it's way deeper than that. You were full of shit from the very beginning, you lied about simple shit. I didn't care what kind of car you drove as long as you had a car. You make great money, babe, and it seemed like you wanted to compare salaries."

"Kai, you know-"

"No, let me finish, Malachi. I told you I wanted a relationship when we first met. You learned about my past, but you used it against me. We fell in love. We loved each other, then you started moving funny like you wanted your cake and ate it too. I did fall back. I fell back real hard, but you didn't fight for it, you didn't fight for the relationship, it's like you just didn't give a fuck, but as soon as I said, let's just fuck, it was great then, so I put you in a box, and I left you there, now all of a sudden you're this prince charming."

"Kai, yes, I was wrong. Yes, I fucked up, but this will be different. I promise to think about it, babe. Please, Kai, I need you. I want you. I wanna wake up next to you someday."

"I hear you, babe. I hear you. This was amazing. I miss you."

I've missed this guy as I kiss him and look into his eyes. This man is really coming for me. I wanted this for so long, but yes, let's just say bad timing, fuck, what about Michael? Do I entertain him? Shit, this is some Y&R shit.

This man helped me out of the shower. Wrapped my towel around my body and said, "Go lay on the bed since your meeting is later. I have time to rub you down with oils and massage your body."

"Oh babe, you're amazing. Thank you!" I said. As I was enjoying this massage, my phone was ringing. I said, "Oh my God! Can't I just enjoy this massage?" But it could be the client, so I grabbed my phone. It was a private number.

"Oh, hell no! Not answering, I had enough shenanigans last night. I'm enjoying this time with him right now. No time for bullshit before work. Fuck that shit."

Malachi said, "Yes, babe, don't hurt me. What are you saying, babe?" "Just what the fuck" I said.

"So does that mean you wanna be my woman?"

"I don't know what I want just yet. All I know is I said don't hurt me." He got quiet.

"Why the fuck you get quiet? What the fuck is the issue?" "Nothing, hun. I'm admiring this beautiful ass body you have shit."

"Oh, shut up and kiss me. I gotta get up and start getting ready. This was amazing today, thank you."

"Can I see you tonight?" I looked at the body language, and he was so hesitant, so I said, "What the fuck is the problem? So this is the shit I'm talking about. I give you what you want, but it's bullshit when I want it. And when I want it…"

"Calm down, Kai!" He said, "I have to look at my schedule to make sure I'm not covering another manager tonight.

"Yeah, whatever, I gotta get ready. See ya yourself out. Have a good day," I said.

"So your attitude just went to trash. What the fuck happened just that fast?"

"Bye, Malachi, I feel like you're selling me some bullshit. So have a good day."

"Kai, stop this stupid bullshit. This what you always do."

"This shit, when I want your time on my time, why just give in to me? Give me what I want and need sometimes. Fuck it, it's thirsty Thursday anyway. I'm a fuck with my girls tonight. Forget it,"

"But Kai..."

"Nope, I'm good. Thanks for the amazing morning sex. It was much needed."

As I was getting ready, my phone kept ringing.

"All them calls, you better get that it's probably that light skin Negro with the crooked hairline."

All I could do was laugh. I said, "You sound a little jealous if I can say so myself. If you asked me.."

"Well, I didn't, so don't play with me KaiAndra."

"Bye Negro; you need to check your schedules or whatever."

"I ordered breakfast from your favorite café. It will be delivered to your job in 30 to 45 minutes. I really love you, woman."

"OK blah blah blah whomp whomp whomp, I hear you bye." I hear the door slam. Guess he's mad... who the fuck does he think he is like, you come over, fuck me good, eat my pussy, wash my body, feed me my favorite breakfast, and I get bullshit excuses about tonight; spending time, man fuck you.

Chapter 6
Business mixed with Pleasure

"Hello?" "damn, how many times you gonna keep calling my phone? Shit." "Well, good morning to you too, babe."

"Michael, what is it? What do you want? I told you I will call you later."

"Fuck, KaiAndra, it's later."

"Well, Michael, I'm not on your time. I'm on my mind, so good day." Click.

These negros got some damn nerves thinking my life revolves around them. Nope, sure it doesn't. Who the fuck again, do they think they are? Anyways, I have to look super sexy today, so I pulled out my blue suit with my pink blouse and pink pumps, with my pink bracelet set. My girl made that. That bitch, is so talented. She's going to the top. As I'm getting dressed, my girls FaceTime me, "Bitch, heffa, where are you? Been calling you or FaceTiming you all night. We were gonna come over there to see what the fuck is going on."

"Oh my God, you won't believe this shit, but I can't talk now, I'm running late. We can tonight over some strong-ass margaritas and Mexican food. Love y'all, chow." Time flies when you're having fun. As I'm leaving my condo, setting the alarm, I'm walking to my parking garage. I hear my phone ringing again. I can't believe this. My hands are full: laptop bag, purse, coffee, and keys.

Fuck it, it'll just have to go to voicemail until I get to the car. Shit, it's probably Michael anyways. I'm filling the car, it's beautiful this morning, birds chirping, shining. My phone rings again. It's him, Malachi. I was hesitant to answer because of how shit went left this morning.

Good sex, good dick, great foreplay, and then we leave attitudes. But my soft-ass answers. "Kaiandra Barnes," in a smart-ass way, actually. He says, "Stop it."

So I replied, "Why, same bullshit, different day."

"I love you, Kandra. Dammit, just love me." I stay silent. "I love you and cater to your needs, babe. I got this," He continued.

"I know you're still there; I hear you breathing." I tried not to laugh, but I did chuckle. "Okay, I gotta go, we'll talk Saturday."

He was huffing, "It's only Thursday." I replied, "But you gotta go over your shifts, right? And I have an executive meeting in a few minutes. Goodbye, sweetheart." Click.

As I'm sitting in traffic, thinking about all that has occurred in less than 12 hours, what is a bitch gonna do? I love him. Do I love Michael? Yes, but I'm not in love with him anymore, to be honest. Not sure if I'm willing to try again with him. That was a lot of hurt, and it kinda, it did fuck me up."

That's where I had a rough patch with him. I was healed with him, Malachi, but it started off so boring. I had to break his shell wide open if you know what I mean. Pulling up to the office, I was thinking to myself, 'He knocked this meeting out of the ballpark, now this client, and keeps succeeding. You got this.'

"Lipstick, check. Hair intact, check. Skirt pulled down, check. Notes and laptop, check. Here we go, black girl magic, sell yourself, Kandra, nail this client to bring your business to the top." I walk into the room and begin.

"Hello, everyone. Thank you for joining us this morning. It's a great day to talk numbers. I am Keondra Barnes."

As I take in the room. I couldn't believe myself. You won't believe who was in this fucking meeting. Are you shitting me? This has got to be some fucking joke.

Michael fucking Washington? What kind of games is this man playing now? Ashton Kutcher, please come out now and say I'm getting pumped. Oh my God, OMG, I'm speechless. So as the meeting starts, this man, Negro, Michael, says, 'Hello, Keondra. I'm Michael Washington, and I'm interested in your company to be an investor, a silent investor, actually, and in your marketing, as your marketing distributor."

"I read your pitch online, myself and my partners were very pleased. We have drawn up some numbers. Let us know if you like our numbers." In my head, I'm like, 'What kind of games is this man playing with me? Fuck, fuck, fuck.' "Okay, Mr. Washington, I'll look this over with my partners and get back to you in a day or two. Thank you for coming, and we'll be in touch."

As I'm packing up my laptop, everyone's leaving but Michael. I'm not surprised, "Babe." "No, sir, I'm at work. I keep it 1000 professional. 100+ professional,"

"Kandra. Don't be upset. I wanted to tell you, but I knew you wouldn't approve because of our relationship."

"We don't have a relationship, Michael." "You know what I mean, Kandra, our past."

"Look, this is a great idea and opportunity for both companies. Just work with me. Like I said in the meeting, I'll be in touch."

"Kai, can we talk in your office, please?" "About what? There's nobody in here." "Just yes or no."

"Okay, follow me."

"Wow, your office is amazing, carpeting everything. I see you, Miss Executive."

"What do you want?"

"Come here, I'm not going to bite you," "Michael. I'm at work."

"Come here." As I'm walking towards him, I know this is dangerous. He's looking good as fuck, smells good. I'm a sucker for a smelling good man.

He pulls me close, hugs me, and whispers in my ear, "I love you, woman, and I'm going to show you every day of my life until you believe me, starting with today. Lock your door and come back to me." Shit, I should've just said no about him coming to my office, but I listened to him, "Lock the door." "What, Michael?" "Come here, baby." "Okay," he kisses me.

Oh my God, how I missed those kisses. Something about them makes me melt and get wet all over, all hot and bothered as well. Laugh out loud, I pull away. "What's wrong?" He asked. I answer, "I'm at work." He adds, "And you're in a meeting. I asked your assistant to clear your books or your schedule for the next hour. You're all mine, baby."

"I know you love sex." As he's unzipping my skirt, whispering in my ear, "I'm going to suck on that pussy until you come, then I'm going to fuck you on top of your desk until you come all over me. And the best part is, we can watch with that big ass mirror that's next to your door."

"But, but, but, no, but-"

"Babe, I got you. Just relax and enjoy the pleasure."

Oh my God, this man has lost it. He gets me open as fuck every time. Oh my God, this feels so good. His lips are making love to my pussy. What the fuck, sex this morning with him, Malachi, then afternoon with Michael? Oh my God, this is that freak hoe shit. Shit, oh my God, really, Kandra? Fuck. Oh shit, I'm about to come. Oh, he's saying, "Come on my lips, baby," as my body is getting hot. I'm grabbing my breasts, squeezing them nipples softly since they are pierced, screaming, "Shit, she's about to come. Fuck, why are you doing this? Oh fuck me, just fuck me, put that dick in me."

"The magnum is on the desk, put it on and fuck me like you missed me." He places that condom on and pushes his 9 inches in my pussy. I'm almost screaming; that felt so good. Fuck, I can't believe I was fucking this man again after all these years in my office at work at that. He's fucking me, saying, "This will be mine forever. This is my pussy." Oh my God, I'm not even paying him attention. He feels so good, goddammit.

As we're both into this hot, steamy office sex, I feel like we are about to both come together. We both are moaning and softly screaming, "Yes, fuck me, oh my God," I'm being a classified hoe today, laugh out loud. As we both come, he slowly pulls out and pushes me back on my desk, and eats my pussy some more.

I told him, "No, you will not digitize me like this anymore today. I will not allow this," chuckle, chuckle. He starts laughing, "Okay, babe, you're lucky you're at work, but I'm not finished with you tonight. Can I see you?" Fuck, how can I say no? "Yes, well, after I meet with the girls after thirsty Thursday." "Really," he says, "you see them all the time, and you really left me." "I've been here, I didn't leave you did." "Okay, smartass, I'll come about 11-ish."

"No, I'll call you, Kai, don't play with me."

"Oh, like how you played with me over and over in several years, yeah, whatever, get out. I have to work before I head out, but thank you, that was amazing, like old times. I could've been your wife by now, but never mind." What the fuck went down in my office? Oh my God, what the fuck just went down this morning?

These men have really fucking lost it, but I love it here, the fuck, I've wanted these last few years. Wait a minute, before you think I'm about that Polly life, no, I'm not. I wanted a life with Michael. I wanted a family, a house, kids, etc. But he chose differently. I was crushed, hell yeah, did I move on, kinda, but was stuck in the, I know he's coming back, he didn't until now.

Well, I get this man again. Well, I want this man again. Why? I fell in love with this man again, I don't know, that pain hit differently for me. I must say today was a very awesome, productive day. Amen. Let the church say amen. Lord, forgive me for my sins. Shaking my head as I wrap up my day, my phone rings, the girls' crazy asses.

"What's up, heffa? Are we meeting at the Mexican spot or what for thirsty Thursday?" "Yes, we are, I'm leaving the office now." "Be safe, see y'all soon. Love y'all, bye." I hung up.

I packed up my laptop, paperwork, grabbed my purse, and headed to the door. And, of course, my phone rings. I huff as I throw my hand in the bag. I gotta get me some new earbuds, Apple buds, beats, pumps, whatever, because this digging for my phone and these big-ass purses sucks. I managed to grab it, and it was him, Malachi. I didn't answer it; I let it go to voicemail. He really pissed me off today, and I had to really think. I'm going to put him on ice for a few hours. I said a few hours, y'all. Damn, finally, I hit the garage and walked to my truck.

Oh my God, you won't believe this shit. My car is covered in my favorite fucking flowers, covered in pink roses and lilies, my favorite flowers. Oh my gosh, oh my God, this is so sweet. But man, and of course, there is no card. Men play games, too, y'all. Was it him, or was it Michael? Who else could it be?"

I'm grabbing all the flowers off my truck and putting them in my car. I felt that someone was standing behind me. I was right. "Oh shit, you scared me. Are you—you're crazy for sneaking up on me. I could've shot you,"

"ha ha," he said. "You probably would have enjoyed that as mad as you were at me this morning." I'm sure you can guess who it is, him, Malachi.

Yes, I know, I'm a sucker. This man melts my inner me, makes me smile, and makes my body sing in so many ways, but his mommy issues really showing him. "Oh my God, you did all this for me, why babe?"

"I felt bad because you're right. I need to stop being selfish and put you first sometimes," "Not so much first, babe, but a priority."

"You're right, Kai. I love you, and I wanna show you how much, and I'm for real, babe."

"Let me show you right now. Hop in the back and let me hide that skirt up. Let my lips touch that sauce, that scrumptious pussy. I love to taste." Oh my God, no, I can't have him, no, thinking to myself. Oh my God, that would be so great. But now, I can't have him all up in my pussy, and I just got my ass fucked earlier. What the fuck, but his hands are the bomb, and before I could say anything, I did freshen up and change panties. This gal's always prepared.

"I just fucking love it there, Keondra." "Yes, babe,"

"What's the problem?"

"Nothing, babe, sorry, I was just daydreaming."

"Babe, can we do a rain check? I'm meeting the girls, and honestly, I'm late. That's probably them calling now."

"Okay, so tonight, like you asked me." Is he fucking kidding? Now, he wants to continue and confirm tonight, and I have Michael coming. Fuck, fuck, click on your feet. Hell, well, fuck, "well, babe, I made plans, I'm chilling with the girls tonight. Let's just stick with Saturday at eight."

"So you want me to wait two days to see you, kiss you, touch you, look at you, fuck you? Are you serious? You're kidding, right?"

"No, actually, I'm not. I asked you earlier, and you couldn't give me the right answer. So honestly, it would be good for us. Give me a kiss; I gotta go. I love the flowers and you, but I really gotta go."

"Okay, sweetie. Give me some more kisses with that tongue. You always make my dick hard when you kiss me. I always want you, Kai. Always."

My ways were fucked up, I know, I know. "Let's talk about this later. Love you."

As I jumped in my truck, my phone was blowing up late as fuck, as usual. I answer and tell my girls, "I'm coming, y'all. Damn, I'm coming."

"What the fuck is taking your ass so long? It's like 10 minutes from your office." "I'll tell you when I get there, okay? See y'all in five minutes or less. Order me a Casamigos strawberry margarita and a shot."

"Wow, bitch. Okay," I hung up.

Chapter 7
Thirsty Thursday

I pull up to our favorite Mexican restaurant, where my girls have been waiting on me.

"Hey, heffas, I finally made it," Keshawn, my girl from middle school, exclaims. "Finally! Come bring your ass here. Where is this glow coming from? I can't wait to hear this shit," she chuckles. Chuckle, Kassidy, the Charmer, and my girl from college, "OK bitch, you sitting down? Your drink is at the table. Spill the fucking tea."

"OK, OK, y'all, fuck, where do I start? Let's take a shot. Cheers! Fuck, I needed that shit. Y'all, Michael Washington is home, and I'm not sure why, but he says he's home for me. He was crazy as fuck at my condo last night, early a.m. Y'all know I've been seeing and fucking him, Malachi, for the last two years and loving every second, minute, hour, etc. But, as I told you, he doesn't want no woman. He likes just fucking me. I mean, my pussy is good, lol," "but mama issues, woo, too much Kai."

"What Kassidy?"

"I mean, men don't want relationships anymore, but consistency is the shit."

"That's it. It's not consistent. Well, it wasn't until Michael showed up." Keashawn screams, "Bitch, what? Come on with the dates, the details!"

"OK, so I was leaving work yesterday and had dick on my mind. Well, him, Malachi, texted me. I didn't respond fast enough, so he called. We set up our night at about 11 PM. Before all of that, Michael was blowing up my phone but private, so I answered and was like, 'Who is this?' He's like, 'Hey babe, I want to see you. You can come here, I'll come to you.' I told him no, when I'm ready, I will call you and hang up.

"Kai, what?"

"Keshawn, that man broke my heart and shattered it, remember? Or did you seem to forget, bitch?"

"No, bitch, I remember your ass in my guest bedroom for a week with your Casamigos," she chuckled.

"OK then, shut the fuck up, like you'd act like you don't remember. So, anyways, I hung up. This Nigga shows up at my door as him, Malachi, was in parking in my parking garage at the house, Kassidy."

"You're kidding, what the fuck?"

"No, he was. I'm not. I was like, 'Oh my God, oh my God!'" "Keshawn, bitch, you single?"

"Yes, but still, I don't want any drama." "The fuck, Keshawn?"

"Yeah, you're right. So, what happened?" They both ask with big eyes. "So, he comes up, saying, 'babe, you are looking so damn sexy. Fuck, who is this?' Before I could say shit, Michael was like, 'I'm so sorry to disturb y'all. I must have the wrong condo or building for my sister. So sorry to disturb you all, you all have a good night.'"

"Y'all, I was shocked as fuck, ladies. I went on about my business. Myself and him, Malachi had an amazing night. I mean, haven't had any dick in weeks, he was playing. Oh my God, Keshawn,"

"no way,"

"it gets better."

"Shut the fuck up, there's more?"

"Yes, so after an amazing session with my fuck buddy, I am walking him out, this man standing at my door. Y'all, fine as fuck, smelling good at 3 AM, with us all standing at the door."

"Him, Malachi, introduces himself, but wait, when Malachi and I were fucking, he said, 'I know that was Michael Washington.' He blew me away, like how the fuck did he know? But I played it cool." Kassidy is screaming, "Kai, what the fuck? Oh my God, that's fucking insane. What happened?"

"They were cool, him, Malachi, left, kissed me passionately, and left.

Mike didn't leave. We talked, but I sent Michael home after his bullshit." "I miss your shenanigans, Kai,"

"What Keshawn?"

"you didn't give Michael none,"

"no, not that night, lol. But I fucked him today in my office, and it was hot, steamy sex. Adrenaline was just going, and it was awesome."

"Kai, what?"

"Kassidy, Kassidy, girl, this is some Tubi shed, Baja hahaha," "shut up. I know it gets better."

"So, him, Malachi, never comes over to my house unannounced. This morning, he does, and fucks my soul and body, orders me breakfast, and has it delivered to my job when I get there, but wait, I need more drinks. Have us order another round."

"So, y'all know, I had a meeting with two business executives this morning, bitches. It was Michael Washington and his business partner who invested in my business and dropped me a check for half a million for a marketing strategy. I was like, what the fuck, oh my God, this man is really amazing, but bitches, I can't get the way he left me and never came back for me. What Keshawn? Why the shaking of your head?"

"Kai, what the fuck are you gonna do?

"Fuck, I don't know him. Malachi showed up at the job, decorated my fucking truck with my favorite flowers, and was trying to kiss me and eat my pussy in the garage before I got here. That's why I was like, I'm running late."

"Kai, oh my God,"

"I know, Kassidy, what the fuck am I gonna do, y'all, let's drink these shots."

"Cheers, oh shit, oh shit, what the fuck you said, Keshawn?"

"So, I asked Michael to come over tonight and denied Malachi, him. Help me, help us. I love a man who has mommy issues and is so materialistic, has a great job, and shows signs of an active father, but there's always that, but then there's Michael Washington, smart, sexy, business-minded, no kids. I'm not in love with him anymore, y'all, but I do love him," shaking my head, I continued, "I feel like he's on a mission or has a secret agenda."

"Well, if he's coming over tonight, ask him, Keshawn, girl, this is some crazy-ass shit."

"Honestly, my opinion, fuck Michael, he had his chance and fucked it up. I will make things work with him, Malachi,"

"He's showing he really loves you and trying to change. That's big for a man. That's just my opinion, though, your life is mad crazy just in 24 hours, adventurous."

"Honestly, my phone is vibrating so much, and it fell off the table," "Damn heifer, which one is it now?" Asked Kassie, I sighed, "It's

Michael," We asked for the check after these last rounds. "Keshawn, so what are you gonna do?"

"Bitch, I'm not sure. I'mma find out what Michael is up to with myself and my business. As far as him, Malachi, I'mma play along and humor him to see if he really wants to share life with me. I really love him and see if life with him is really what it is, to see if he's really changed and going to change. People do change, y'all."

Keshawn and Kassidy both laugh. "Yeah, OK, bitch, if you say so," Kassidy remarks. I called Michael back as we settled the check. "Hey," I spoke once he picked up.

"Hey, haven't heard from you since I laid you out on your desk this morning. Is everything OK?"

"Yes, thanks for the reminder. It was great, though."

"Yes, I'm leaving my girls now. Can you come and meet me at my condo in about, let's say, 45 minutes?"

"'OK, let's say an hour." "OK, bye."

Keshawn asked, "What did he say?" "He said OK," I replied. "You gonna fuck him again?"

"Damn girl, all up in the Kool-Aid," Kassie yelled out. "I know, right? Damn, I don't know."

"Shit, I'm single, right?" "Kai what? Just be careful,"

"Duh, always. I'm leaving, girls. My phone is ringing off the hook." I look at my navigation. It's him, Malachi.

"Hey, babe, what's up?" he sounds off. "Hey, where are you?" "I'm leaving the girls, what's up?"

"OK, normally you text me or something. I was just a little concerned, baby. I just left you. Do you see the time?" he asked.

"Negro, it's 9:30 PM."

"Yes, and I'm not your child, so stop treating me like I'm one of yours."

"You know what, good night, we will talk tomorrow." I hung up. Click. Of course, he calls back. I don't answer. I don't want no bullshit. Damn, he calls again, and this time I answer.

"What, baby, what?"

"I'm sorry, you're right. I love you. I don't wanna fight."

"Then don't come to me like that and start no bullshit. I was out with my girls, I had an amazing time, don't kill my vibe."

"I understand, get home safe. I love you, and if you can't, let me know, and if you can, let me know you made it home safe. Thank you."

"OK, babe." Finally home, fucking home. God!

Chapter 8
Michael Washington

Wow, what a day! Woo, I can't complain. It was absolutely fabulous. The house smells good, still tidy from yesterday. I'm definitely winning tonight. I'm going to take a nice candle-lit bath with some sea salt, pomegranate beads, and scented candles. I like bubbles too, as I'm running my water. I slip off my suit, hanging it up, and turning on my speaker to jazz.

By this time, I'm fully naked, about to step into my tub full of bubbles. It smells great; the candles light up the bathroom. With them lit, I hear a knock at the door. Damn, is it time already? Where did that hour go? It can't be 11. As I grab my phone, it's 11:05. It's Michael. Fuck, I wanted this time to soak and think about what's happening. Why is this man here? I'm yelling as he can hear me.

"I'm coming," the doorbell rings. "Like, okay, damn, I'm coming." I forgot to grab a towel as if he hadn't seen me naked before. I open the door slightly. It's his fine ass, woof, Mr. Michael Washington. As I slightly open the door, he says, "Damn, baby, you are so fine. Your body is gorgeous, just banging. Jesus, woo," I'm blushing.

"Oh, shut up, come in, close the door. I was about to soak and relax in the tub." He asked, "Can I join?" "Let me get in first and enjoy my hot water, then I'll cool it down, and then you can join me." "Of course," he says. "Woman, let me take care of you tonight. Let me wash your body from head to toe, thighs, your pussy, your breasts, everything. OK?"

"OK, come on," as I slid into my hot water.

I see his dick through his gray sweatpants; it's rock-hard. I wasn't going to say anything, but he caught me staring. Chuckling, he says. "Yes, my dick is hard, baby. You turn me on every time I see you; I can't help it." I change the subject real quick because I really want to know why the fuck this man is here and getting into my feelings all involved and trying again.

"So, Michael, Mr. Washington, what's your game? Why are you really here? What are you up to? And why now?" His response was, "Damn, just straight like that. Yes, Negro, why are you here?" He tries to be smooth and grabs my washcloth, lathers it up with my Dove soap body wash, and states, "Massaging my legs and thighs and watches me close my eyes and relax."

"Will you ask, Kai? I'm here to expand your business on the West Coast. You have the best marketing strategy in the US right now, and it will be good for us to do business together. And in the meantime, we get to learn each other all over again and possibly fall in love with each other again. That's a chance I want to take with you, and I hope you'll think about taking that chance with me. If you fall in love with me again, I'll never stop. I've never stopped before." Before I can answer, he's up to my breasts, caressing them, and that's the spot to turn me on. All I could do was moan, but he knew what he was doing.

"OK, OK, I want to talk about this. I know what you're doing, Mr. Washington." "What am I doing, Kai?" "You're turning me on to fuck you and have another session. What, was that so bad?" He asked. "No, but yes, I want to keep talking. So, did you really invite me over to talk?" "Yes, Michael, I did," my serious face open, my eyes raised up, and yeah, "yes, I truly did. I gave you years, and you threw that shit away like it wasn't shit."

A tear ran down my face as he wiped it. "Babe, I know I hurt you. I hurt us. I can't apologize enough." "Sometimes, it's not about an apology." I watched his expression and body language. I could tell he was hurt from what I said, but I didn't give a fuck. Shit, I waited days, weeks, months, fuck, two years for him to come and apologize to me and put a ring on me. Nothing. Then, four years later, he thinks he could just show up. "Baby, I miss you." "Get the fuck out of here, nope, Michael," he cuts me off. "Shush, baby, let me do this." As he washes my arms and tells me to turn over, as he washes my back, my fat ass, I feel him getting into the water with me.

"Damn, this shit is hot," making me laugh as he rubs my shoulders, my back, caresses my ass. "Baby, just relax, I know I hurt you, Kai, I'm sorry. Let me show you how much I love you and never stop." "Michael, baby," I felt him kissing my neck and my ears. "I love you, Kai," as he whispers, "I love you, you're my baby, just let me show you." Oh my God, his body felt so good, and his touch against mine. But all I could think about was him, Malachi, how he had been changing and trying to get his life together for him to love me the way I needed. I really love him. I fell in love with him after our second date. We had a picnic at an all-exclusive park by the ocean. It was so amazing; he showed me he really cared about me.

"Kai, hello, are you there?" "Sorry, I must have gone into a daydream." "What did you say, Michael?" "Never mind." "OK, why are you ready to get out? I'm pretty exhausted. Today was very unexpected but fun." "Well, it's not over yet," as he says, "the night just began, huh?" "What are you talking about, Mr. Washington?" I asked, like, "What the fuck now?" "Cho, Cho, Kai, come, oh baby, get out. I want to suck on that pussy and make you come and relax yourself. You're still very uptight, Michael, woman, stop talking, damn, come on."

I knew he wasn't going to approve whatever I had to say, so I did, I got out. He wrapped me up and picked me up and laid me across my bed, dried my body off, and kissed my thighs and legs up to my pussy. He kissed my lips, so soft, with so much enthusiasm. All I liked to do was lay back and enjoy him. It was so good; oh my God, OMG. I didn't realize I screamed. He said, "Yes, babe, enjoy it." I was so into it. I said, "Come, fuck me, fuck me so good till she comes and soaks the sheets." I saw him push inside softly. "Give me all of you right now, harder, harder," as he did. I began to moan, "Shit, fuck yes, harder, fuck me." He grabs my breast, sucks on it, teases my nipples, and my nipple rings with his tongue.

"Fuck, Michael, why are you here fucking with my head and my feelings?" I feel his dick getting harder as he's fucking me. I hear him say, "I want you too, oh my God, I'm about to come," and he says, "Let's come together," as we both scream, "Fuck, fuck, we came."

I know my neighbors are like, "What the fuck?" That's the most excitement they heard from me in months. Chuckle, chuckle, as Michael got up. I remember him saying he wanted something, so I asked, "Michael, what were you saying you wanted?" He said, "Nothing, baby, when the time is right, I'll tell you." "OK, well, were you gonna stay the night and cuddle?" "Oh, I'm allowed to stay the night, Negro, shut the fuck up, are you or aren't you? Because I was gonna say, let's take the rest of that bottle of Casamigos and call it a night." "Yes, I'll stay and cuddle that sexy ass and body. Lord, what did I just do? Fuck, why do I be so needy?"

As we took our drinks to my living room, I heard his phone vibrating. Of course, my smart ass is gonna say, "Oh, was that your lover or your woman calling, Kai?" "What?" he says, "No, smart ass, it's your mother-in-law." I'm like, "Stop it, at 1:30 AM?" He said, "Yes, I make her check-in before she gets in bed. That's the only agreement we have if she wants to continue to live alone; she had a stroke a few years ago." "Oh, let me talk to her." "Hey, Mrs. Washington, Kai, is that that sweet, high-pitched voice of yours?" "Chuckle, chuckle, yes, ma'am. How is my sweet daughter and love doing?" "I'm just wonderful. How are you?" "Well, I'm making it. My son thinks he is my daddy, but I'm grateful for a son that cares. I hope to see you sooner than later, young lady. I love you; tell that son of mine. Goodnight." "Yes, ma'am, will do. I love you, too. Goodnight," click.

"Michael, yes, baby?" "Nothing, are you ready to go to bed?" He says, "No, Kai, I want to know about..." "Oh, shit, here it is, here we go. He's gonna ask about him. Malachi, Mr. Washington, not now, not right now. We just fucked, and it was amazing. We had some drinks, not tonight." "Dammit, Kandra, why not? Why not now?" "Wow, really? Who do you think you are? I'm sorry, babe, it's just..." "Michael, goodnight. Matter-of-fact, I'll sleep alone; blankets are behind the couch, Kai, no, goodnight. I'm not doing this with you tonight. We just had a good night, and you fucked it up in seconds. Fuck, I knew that he was going to ask, but we just had a great sex session. It was amazing; the man ate the shit out of my pussy and put the pipe down. Now, we're over here arguing 'cause I know what he's going to ask. I'm not talking about him tonight."

Chapter 9
Funky Attitude

Shit, good night! Alarms are ringing off the hook, shit. OK, damn, I have the most annoying alarm clock to get my ass up. Woo, I'm yawning and shit, feeling good. Bitch loves sex, and I got some good dick these last two days in a week. It was quiet; I didn't hear Michael or whatever in the living room. I got up and put on my robe to discover he was gone. Wow, that's what we're doing? Woo, these men, see, this is the shit I'm talking about. Whatever, let me get my day started. I am about to start my shower, start the coffee pot, and proceed to go to my closet.

What the fuck am I gonna wear today? I'm feeling a little bright but chill. I'm gonna put on my mustard blazer, some jeans, and some pumps. As I'm about to jump in the shower, my phone vibrates. It's him, Malachi. "Good morning, gorgeous" "Hey, babe, I slept amazingly, like a baby." "You must have. You didn't call me or text me and let me know." "You got it, OK? Oh my God, baby, I'm so sorry, my bath was so relaxing, I almost fell asleep in it." "OK, well, I just wanted to tell you I love you. I'm holding on tight, high. You're my person and my reason." "Oh shit, this is getting deep, Kai." "Yes, babe, thank you for believing in me, thank you for another chance that you're even considering, always, babe. Have an amazing day. Talk to you later." "You too, sweetheart, can't wait until Saturday." He hangs up. Oh my God, why is this my life right now? Is this really happening?

As I'm getting dressed, and I must admit, bitch can dress. OK, coffee, check, laptop bag, check, Brahman, check, I'm walking out of my condo. Here comes chatty Kathy, my neighbor, Melinda, "You had some night, huh?" Her nosy ass, "Yes, as a matter of fact, I did. You should try fucking your husband and sucking his dick, and maybe you could have some excellent stories and exciting noises coming from your condo. Should I? Have a great day."

So as I'm driving to work, I'm still amazed how this man just got up and walked the fuck out of my house and didn't speak all because I didn't wanna talk about him, Malachi. Is he fucking serious? Like, I really wanna call him up and be like, so this is the bullshit we are now? But I'm gonna stay silent, chill because I am good at bullshit too, and this is the shit I'm talking about. How do you think you're just gonna pop up four years later and think I'll just bow down to your weak-ass apology and be your *yes girl*? Who the fuck does this man think he is?

"Fuck that, speak of the fucking devil. It's his punk ass calling me now. I was hesitant to answer honestly, but I want to know the fucking reason his ass left."

"Hello?" Yep, I answered all dry with an attitude, gonna come over, caress my body, bathe me, fuck my ass. Fuck me good as hell, then catch an attitude.

"Hello, yes, Michael."

"Well, good morning to you, Miss Barnes." "Yep, what can I do for you, Mr. Washington?"

"I see you have an attitude, and I'm assuming because I left and didn't speak or tell you."

"I guess you're right. What do you want, Michael, you are into these bullshit games, and all honestly, I'm too busy for your shenanigans this morning."

"Kandra, what Negro, I hate when you're like this."

"Well, what did you do to put me there? Oh, that's right, you left on bullshit."

"OK, you're right. I was in my feelings and bounced as soon as I heard you asleep, sound asleep actually from that dick I put in you."

"Yeah, whatever, and your feelings about what, him, Malachi?"

"Wow, because after we fucked, you wanted to pillow talk about a man who has entered my life and whatnot, Michael. That wasn't the best time or timing to talk about that situation. I mean, lately, your timing has been really shitty, I'll give you that."

"Yeah, whatever, so when can we talk about that situation?"

"What situation, him, Malachi, that Negro isn't a situation, so you say, how is he? Explain; because I'm fucking and sucking him with no strings these last two years, it's complicated but not a situation. We know where we stand with each other."

"Oh, OK, and you're comfortable with that shit at 45?" "Wow, so you're judging me now?"

"If you call it that, Kai, then I guess so. I'm not about to have this conversation with you right now. I'm on my way to the office."

"OK, and I'm trying to have a beautiful, successful day. I'm hanging up now, Kai." "Don't hang up this phone. This conversation is not done."

"It is for me. We need to talk. I am in love with you, my life is in circles without you, I need to talk on a serious note so I can proceed with my plans."

"Michael, yes, babe, what plans? We need to talk on a serious note, no bullshit, no sex, etc."

"Fine, when are you free?"

"Well, Miss Executive, I should ask you. When are you free?"

"Let me check my calendar and get back to you so you can have my full, undivided attention. Here you go with the extra bullshit, whatever. I will call you soon and let you know. I do have a life outside of work. Bye, Michael. Have an amazing day."

"Damn, I love you, why can I get that? We aren't there, Michael, and trust me, you did for years, I know, I know, I fucked up. I'll be waiting for your call, sweetheart. Bye, yeah, bye, that man still gets under my skin."

"Shit, what the fuck am I gonna do? I need to figure this shit out before it gets messy and someone gets hurt. I can admit the attention is fucking amazing."

"Woo, work has been amazing today, it's Friday. Hell, yes, ready for the motherfucking weekend. Dinner with him, Malachi, I gotta admit, this man is really doing a great job with change and showing me he really wants us to work. Deep down, I want to believe him. I really want him to love with his heart and not his wallet. Fuck materialistic bullshit, that's not love. These women nowadays want that fake love, that bullshit. Like I said, I want Cinderella-type shit, Brock and Michelle, or Bonnie and Clyde. We shall see what our future holds. Only time will tell."

"Wrapping up my day at the office, about to head home and see what will be popping tonight. Thought about hitting up the girls, but Kassidy has a date with a mystery man, in case Sean is out of town until Sunday, out chasing a dream. Shit, I am mad at her ass; I like out of town. It, too, laugh out loud, the suspense and adrenaline of seeing each other after weeks."

So, here I am, getting ready for the weekend, unsure of what it holds. Michael's call has left me feeling some type of way, but I'm not about to let it ruin my vibe. I'll deal with him when the time comes. For now, it's all about enjoying the moment and seeing where life takes me.

As I walk into my condo, I can't help but feel a sense of excitement for the weekend ahead. Despite the drama and uncertainty, there's a part of me that's looking forward to spending time with Malachi and seeing where things go.

But for now, it's time to relax and unwind. I kick off my shoes, pour myself a glass of wine, and sink into the couch. The weekend is here, and I'm ready for whatever it may bring.

Chapter 10
Friday night

I pulled up at my condo, and there was a visitor, of course. I was not sure why these men didn't understand. Don't come over my shit unannounced, like what the fuck! Don't they get that Imma have to get Cardi B or Megan Thee Stallion on them real quick and shit?

"Hey babe, I know you are like, what the fuck is he doing here without calling?"

"Yes, you're absolutely right. What the fuck, Malachi? This has got to stop."

"I haven't seen your face in 24 hours babe, and you haven't talked to me all day nor texted or called."

"I thought that that nig girl captured your heart, and you said fuck me, babe. Really? Let me say this... we aren't together...

"Remember you decided to play my games with me and fall back and shit when I confess my love for you, my heart, etc. Remember KaiAndra?"

"No, you don't get to do this right now." "So what are you saying, Kai?"

"What I'm saying is... I do love you, but things between us have been rocky as fuck, and shit takes time.... this can't be rushed. We have plans tomorrow night. Let's have dinner. Enjoy each other's company and go from there. Give me a kiss and go home."

"Damn! Can't come in?"

"No, Malachi, go home."

Wow, he comes closer to me and kisses me. Oh my God, his kisses are so passionate. He makes my pussy skip beats, fuck that tongue, big lips, and all shew. I pushed him away and said, "OK, babe, I can't wait to see you tomorrow. I love you, and drive safely."

He said, "I love you too, Mrs. Combs."

I was like, "huh?" Like, I didn't hear him say his last name.

He replied, "Nothing, baby, make sure you open that package sometime tonight; I picked it out myself."

I shook my head. This man loves to shop. I said, "OK, honey, thank you!"

I opened my door and picked up this gorgeous box all pretty wrapped. My damn phone was ringing. I was like... well, shit, my phone is off the hook. Who was it? It's Miss Washington. I didn't even know she still had my number. I was thinking, what the fuck could she possibly be wanting? What is Michael up to now?

I answered all sweet. "KaiAndra. Hello, this is Miss Washington. How are you, baby?"

"I'm OK."

"I wanted to talk to you woman to woman. Do you have a minute?" "Yes, ma'am. I always have time for you."

"All for an old lady like me?" She chuckled.

She continued, "Baby. I know Michael has never stopped loving you."

Whoa, this lady ain't changed a bit. Still, throat right to the point. I laughed out loud, "Yes!"

"No, baby, let me finish." "Yes, ma'am."

"But he's realized his mistake, and he's trying to make it right. I know how he handled things in the past. It wasn't the greatest. I got on his ass badly about it. I just knew you were going to be my daughter-in-law already."

"But.."

"No, baby, let me finish." "Yes, ma'am,"

"This man has flown from Kansas City to Tallahassee, Florida, to earn your love and trust back, baby. That's a big deal considering how busy this man is."

"Yes, ma'am, I understand, but..."

"Yes, baby."

"Do you know I waited years, months, weeks, days for him to call me to apologize for leaving me and not looking back? Until now, my heart was broken, devastated. This man I loved, I gave everything to him, just gave up and left for money. It took me a few months to a year to let him go."

"I know that baby. Just let him show you and explain. Enjoy the time. No need to make a decision now, my sweetheart, but give him that opportunity."

"Yes, ma'am."

"I know you Have a new love interest, I heard. Just look at all your options and opportunities before giving up and closing the door completely on him."

"Yes, ma'am."

"Well, let Mama go, baby. I just wanted to talk to you personally. I love you, sweetheart. You call me anytime. Don't let distance separate us again!"

"Yes, ma'am. Goodnight."

Wow, what the fuck was that? So this Negro called his mama and told her I have another love interest, to apply more pressure. Oh my God, let me get my wine out. I think Imma just chill tonight. This is too much.

Negro trying to lay in on the bullshit with his mama... shit.. come on, Michael...

I was sipping my wine while sitting in my theater recliner, opening this big ass box that Malachi brought over. As I opened the box, there was a note written by him.

It reads, "To the love of my life, things started off rocky, but I know what kind of woman you are, and I know what kind of woman I need. And you are her. I don't see myself with anyone else. We are learning from each other and

I definitely want to continue learning with you for more years to come. Please allow me to show you how much. I have purchased this dress for a lovely evening, Saturday night. This jewelry set from your girl to go with it. Yes, baby I pay attention more than you think. I love you, woman. Please let me continue to show you why I need you. I will never give up on us. If you will allow me to love - Malachi."

Wow, this man is showing the fuck out. This has totally warmed my heart. This man has never written me shit; maybe, some text like I love you or "Let's fuck" or "Can you bounce on me tonight?" but never this. Could this be what I have been praying for?

Damn, I killed that glass of wine. Keep pouring, Jefa, I said to myself. Yes, I talk to myself sometimes. Who the fuck doesn't, I chuckled. Saturday encounter with shenanigans.

Oh shit! Did I fall asleep already? Rolling my jeans and tank in my chair. Damn! I guess you can say I was tired. It's been an eventful week. I checked the time. It was 8 AM. Woo! burst-turpin-sun shining through my windows. I looked at my phone. It had 14 missed calls. What the fuck! Who, why? And shaking my head. Damn! Well, let's see Michael Michael Michael. Well, 10 of those were Michael, four of them were Kassidy. Shit! I hoped my girl was OK. Let me call her. I dialed her and went to voicemail.

"Hey girl, sorry I missed your calls. Are you OK? Call me!"

I was going through my text messages. Michael texted, "Baby, are you OK? What's up? Did you check your calendar? OK, Kandra? What the fuck? What did I do now? Oh, let me guess you with that Negro whatever, he definitely don't put the dick on you like me, call me! Love you, good night."

What is wrong with this man? Is he really trying to wash my ass? I got my day started. I was very excited to see Malachi that night. He gets dressed up smelling good, his shiny bald head with his black attire, shit! Yes! Talk about fine dark chocolate with that sexy ass beard. I shook my head. I got my pussy already beaten, meow! I chuckled.

I sent him a text, "Thank you, sweetie, for my gift, but the best part is your letter. I can't wait to see you tonight. PS I hope you can stay the night and keep me company. I love you, sexy love, Kai."

I got a quick response. Wow, definitely not like the past. He responded, "You're welcome, baby. I can't wait either. Yes, I will stay the night with my queen."

Wow! a quick response on that, too. What the fuck! I texted, "I love you too, babe. Enjoy your Saturday."

"I will be there at 8 PM sharp, Malachi." God dammit! Who is this man? Therapy is really working on him in the streets.

"Hey, do I know you?"

"Well, you should, or you just playing like you don't remember me?"

"Well, no, sweetheart, I don't. Are you a fan?" I laughed out loud. It was funny.

"No, Michael Washington's fiancé" "Excuse me bitch! What did you say?" "No, you heard me correctly."

Oh, did this bitch just approach me and say Michael's fiancé? Get the fuck out of here! She's flashing this ring all in my face.

"Well, congrats! Why are you flashing that shit all in my face? I guess congratulations are in order."

"Right, thanks. I know he's coming up to do business with you and all, but he's been gone for two weeks and been super busy, so I thought..." I was surprised.

"Well, that's great. Have a great day." "Wait, what?"

"Well damn! What's your problem?"

"Nothing. I have a time limit on things I need to get done before my date tonight, OK?"

"So Michael didn't tell you we were together?"

"Why would he? He's just here for business..." This Nigga all up in my face fucking and sucking on my pussy, and then has the nerve to be engaged. Is he fucking kidding me? Woo, I am so fucking pissed. I could blow steam, but I definitely ain't about to give this bitch no heat.

"Oh well, considering y'all had history, I thought maybe y'all would have caught up."

"What? You thought wrong." "What's your name, love?"

"Oh, come on, KaiAndra, you saw me in the tabloids and stuff."

"Possibly. Michael changes his women like he does his socks and boxers, seldomly." The fuck she thinks I am a stalker.

"Bitch, I know who the fuck you are, Kim, right?" "Actually, Kimberly."

"Oh, excuse me, Kimberly. Well, congrats again. I must leave you. Take care!" The nerve of this bitch.

"Wait, what... KaiAndra, you don't have to be nasty." "I'm not. Just have things to do."

"Will you be attending our wedding?"

Is this bitch really going to tell his ass to send me an invite? He definitely loves my address.

"Chill, darling!" The look on her face was priceless.

I couldn't wait to get in my truck and call this man but I thought to myself, why be mad? He's not your man, just a girl from your past that ain't shit but a good fuck, but a whole fiancé, though, what the fuck! Why am I mad? Why do I have a lump in my throat? \

The fact that this man has been trying me for these last few days. 'I love you, Cassandra' blah blah... well, fuck him. I need to focus on my day tonight.

Get your shit together bitch, I thought to myself. Get your shit together. I was going to get my makeup done at Macy's, so let me hurry up. It's almost 4 PM this Negro is always late, but I wanna be ready.

My phone was ringing; It was Kassidy, my bestie. "You OK?"

"Yes, babe! I was just checking in. Yes, you better know that out-of-town dick will fuck you up, huh?"

"Hell, yes! Bitch it's been amazing. Had me screaming in tongues, something I love to do."

"Anyways, I was calling for updates." "Oh my God, where do I begin?" "Damn! That's crazy?"

"Yes, girl! Hell, yes!"

"OK, I'll be home tonight for real. Well. I'm going out with Malachi tonight."

"Ooh, girl, that seems to be getting hot and heavy. I'm liking it." "Me too. Ciao, me too."

"We'll see."

"OK, let's talk Sunday."

"OK, I love you."

"Love you too sis. Bye"

My feelings were still fucked up, engaged! But all of this lasted 24 hours... from Michael to Washington engaged... I need a drink, but I need to get my makeup done, and I need to be on time. Let me slide to this liquor store and grab a shot of 1800 tequila real quick. Shit! I can't believe this Negro. How should I feel? Fuck this. This is way too much. My feelings aren't hurt, but I have mixed emotions about all this bullshit. These last few days have been laying thick on my mind, and his ass is engaged. I need to let this go and focus on my business. And this man Malachi, who really wants me for me.

No bullshit! While I'm on my second shot, feeling good and ready to see Malachi. Wow, this heifer beat my face to the gods; I look good. Let me get my ass home, shower, and get dressed.

Chapter 11
Controversy Bullshit

Face beat check! Outfit fitted, check! Damn! This dress, he did good. Damn! I feel sexy, look sexy, and couldn't wait to have a good night with babe.

My phone was ringing, it was Michael. I was not in the mood for no bullshit. No lies... Fuck that man tonight. I left him on voicemail until I was ready to confront him about what happened today.

My phone kept ringing. I definitely put him on DND and then heard knock knock. It must be babe. Hold on, damn! He didn't call me and say he was on his way. Let me check my camera. I ain't with the shits tonight. I looked. Oh, it was babe, looking good as fuck, sharp as attack. Made a lady have a heart attack.

I opened the door, and he smelled so good. Damn smells good, looks good, and that's mine. I get greeted with smooches and a big bear hug. It was absolutely wonderful and so comforting after all the bullshit I experienced this afternoon. I guess you can say, yes, I was bothered, but I felt amazing and looked amazing. Michael, on the other hand, who the fuck he thought he was.

Malachi said, "Damn! Baby, you look amazing. You are so beautiful, and that dress fits you like a glove and hits your curves. Great!"

"Thank you, babe. So where are you going?" He said, "It's a surprise baby. Are you ready?"

"Yes, babe, I sure am. Let me just grab my purse." My phone was still ringing.

"Is this Negro for real, hahaha. His fiancé must have ran back and said she saw me. Who cares? Do I really give a fuck at this point? I don't babe." "Yes, sweetheart. Let's go. We have reservations."

"OK, I'm ready, babe. He's like, "No."

I was like, "You don't know what I'm going to ask you."

He responds, "Yes, I do. Two pictures only, and we gotta go." Haha. I was like, "Wow, you do know me so well. Okay, say cheese."

He never smiles for our photos, but the serious look actually worked this time. My man looks so good. Oops, did I say that? 'My man' I liked the ring of that, woo! He's so fucking sexy, shit! Dark chocolate, his beard, trimmed and schlong, hangs just right, and skin so smooth like chocolate and shiny. I can fuck him right now. Lord have mercy!

We reached the garage, and he opened my door for me. Chivalry still lives here, baby. We were pulling out of the garage, and guess who the fuck pulled up. Mr. Fucking Washington. I saw him pulling in as we were pulling out. Thank God he didn't see me or Malachi, shoo, dodged that bullet. I hope I placed his ass on DND.

Malachi asked, "Sweetie you OK?" I just got quiet.

"Yes, babe! Was just daydreaming about how Imma a suck on your dick tonight." I was quick on my feet; I had to be.

"Damn, baby! Don't make me pull over and give you this dick before we go into the restaurant." He chuckled.

"Do we have time, babe? I really, really could enjoy you right now."

He said, "No, babe. As much as I wish. We have reservations at 9:15 PM."

We were pulling up at the Blue Hollow, one of my favorite restaurants. Oh my God, this man. We got out of the car, and babe started acting weird; all nervous and shit and stiff.

"What the hell is wrong with you?"

Of course, I noticed everything, so I grabbed his face, stared him in his eyes, and told him, "Babe, Relax! I am yours, and you are mine. My focus is rebuilding our love." And kissed him passionately. I can see that relaxed him.

"Thank you, my queen, for that!"

When we entered the restaurant, it had dim lighting; it was so beautiful there, and the setup was so gorgeous. Real fine dining at its best. They saw us in the middle of the restaurant, and the waiter brought over two bottles of wine.

I was like, "Babe, how did you know I love these two wines? Look at you, baby. You really have changed. Damn, what did I do to deserve this?"

"KaiAndra, you've been my rock for these last two years and I'm so grateful for you loving me. How a man should feel."

Yes, God! You are molding this man how I prayed woo! This is new, and I like it. I excused myself to go to the restroom and checked my phone. I saw text messages just came through.

"KaiAndra. What the fuck? I know that crazy bitch approached you talking about we getting married. It's not true, baby. Don't believe the hype. I know you saw me when I pulled in your garage. I followed you in. That Negro... that guy you call, you know, your strings... I know you at that fancy restaurant. I don't give a fuck. I'll come in there. Call me.."

Funny thing is that I know he will, but I don't give a fuck, not tonight. Malachi is showing me he's that man, and I want him. I need him. He brings no drama... he has no drama, and he really loves me. Let me get back before this man thinks I'm taking a shit, I chuckled.

I walked back to the table. I saw my girls and Malachi at the table. I'm blushing, saying oh my God, what is this man up to? My girls were smiling. I finally reached them.

Kassidy and Keshawn were like, "Surprise, friend. Your man called us and told us to show up, you know. We love him."

"What's this all about y'all? What's going on?"

Oh my God, is this man about to propose to me? Oh my God! Oh my God!

So Malachi said, "Babe, I wanted to show you how serious I am about you. I'm not letting go ever again. Let's order!"

My girls were like, "Fuck girl, he's it. He's applying mad pressure." We all started laughing and chuckling.

Malachi said, "Ladies, order whatever. It is on me." The girls were like, "Say less," I shook my head.

They cracked me up, great conversation, good food, and most of all, I was surrounded by people who love me, and I love them, no drama. Time was passing us up and Babe ordered strawberry cheesecake as he knows that's my favorite. No matter where we eat, he always orders it for us to share. This man! This man! How did I get so lucky for this man to choose me and us growing together?

Malachi said, "Excuse me, ladies, can I have your undivided attention, please?" Oh shit, what is this man about to say? What is this man about to do? Fuck! Oh shit, OK! OK! Woo!

"I want to say this woman has loved me through so much bullshit. My asshole antics, my disappearing acts, my late-night work schedule, everything that could come up always comes up. I couldn't have asked for a better understanding, loving no filter, gorgeous, amazing woman like you, Kandra. I know exactly what I want, and I want you, babe, always, forever, and every day. I want you to be in the mood for me every day as I'm in the mood for you every day." My girls were like oh, that's so sweet and cute.

With all that being said, he gets on one knee. Oh my God, this is it! He is really doing this. He's asking me to be his wife...

"KaiAndra, will you do me the honors of being my wife?" Everyone was looking at us at the restaurant, just frozen. It was so quiet you could hear a pin drop.

I was about to give this man my answer, and I heard, "Negro, get up!

Stop looking for an answer 'cause it's hell no!" I was shocked.

"Michael! What are you…" before I could finish, Malachi said, "Excuse you, you are being disrespectful and rude, and you're not invited to this party, so you need to excuse yourself before I surely do it for you."

Kassidy and Keshawn's eyes were as big as gumballs, and mouths so open that a fly could fly in them like mine.

"What the fuck is going on right now?" I spoke too soon on no drama. "Oh my gosh, Michael, what are you doing here?"

"No, why are you here?"

"We are enjoying our evening. And I'm here with friends. And…" "Yeah, I know…your fuck buddy…"

"Stop this bullshit, Michael! Not here, not now. Don't you have a fiancé waiting for you to go home or go to her!"

"Kandra, that is not true. She's a phony. We aren't looking…" "Michael, I'm in the middle of something, as you can see.." "Yeah, I see this full thing. You're gonna marry him."

Malachi said, "What the fuck bro? Brother, you had your chance, and you fucked up. I love her, and she deserves someone to provide leave and court her with loyalty, comfort, friendship, and lots more. I plan on doing that until there is no more breath in my body, so I think you need to excuse yourself."

"Baby, you don't have to explain shit to him.

Michael said, "Oh, so you're gonna do me that way after the intimacy and your office…" Fuck! Is this man for real? Messing with my business.

Keshawn said, "Michael, you need to stop. You need to go!"

Michael said, "Keshawn, mind your business." I looked over at Malachi's face. He was so hurt by what Michael had just said. This is not how I wanted him to find out that I and Michael had slept together in my office.

"Malachi, babe!"

"Stop, Kai, not right now."

"Yeah, she let me taste that sweet pussy and then big breast." "Michael! Stop it! Babe, Malachi. Baby, let's go!"

"Kai babe. Please let me just take care of this bill and I think you should go home with your girls. I need some time to think."

"Baby, please don't do this. I am so sorry. I love you, and I want you." "How can you want me, and you're fucking him at your office. Come on, Kai!" Tears were rolling down my face because I knew better, but the excitement of two men loving on me and wanting me was amazing. Shit girl, I was single, but I didn't want Malachi to get hurt, not this way, not at all this. Malachi was sad. Back to therapy, etc. Fuck! Fuck! Come on, Kai! Kassidy grabbed my purse.

As she grabbed the napkins off the table and drove, she said, "Come on, beautiful. It will be OK, babe."

I yelled out to Malachi, "I love you."

"I love you too, Kandra, but baby, I need some time to adjust to what just happened and what was said," he chuckled.

"Yeah, my boy, she's not yours yet."

"Michael, stop it, please! You have definitely caused enough drama tonight. I'm definitely not in the mood for your shenanigans, and probably not ever. Good night... matter-of-fact, go back to your social media skank. Let's go, Kassidy Keshawn. I'll call you tomorrow."

Micheal said, "Hell no, I'm following you to your house." "We got you, sissy."

"I love y'all. Thank you!" What the fuck just happened.

Chapter 12
Damage Control

I was about to give Malachi an answer, and then boom. Everything went to shit in five minutes. Tears were just rolling down my face, all this pretty make-up ruined. My baby was hurting. I never meant for that to happen. What was I gonna do then?

Michael said, "This is not over, Kai. I love you. Just let me explain." "Fuck you, Michael!"

He said, "You don't mean that." "Oh yes, the fuck I do."

Kassidy said, "Yes, sissy! Can you stop by Maggiano's liquor? I need some tequila, please."

"Yes, sissy!"

The ride home was silent. I just had nothing to say. How could my heart be broken? I was single, but I hurt who was fixing himself to be better for me and him and us, and I probably just fucked all that up.

I can't believe Michael. I've never seen him act that way. What the fuck! Like the fucking nerve! I didn't react when that bitch approached me, but I left with class and all that I don't have, and boom.

I pulled out my phone. Siri! Call Malachi on FaceTime. I'm not giving up. I love Malachi. There is definitely no doubt. He's what I wanted and needed that night. He showed me everything. I got no answer.

"Shit Kassidy!"

"Yes, sis!"

"What the fuck just happened, girl!"

"I have no clue. What the fuck Michael was on. Why did he? How did he even know you were there, girl?"

"I haven't had a chance to call you, some bitch approached me, the bitch that Michael was parading around in Kansas City. His fiancé approached me when I was in the mall."

"Bitch what fiancé?"

"Oh yeah, his... supposedly and get he supposedly engaged had the ring on, etc. In my face, blah blah blah, saying it's good and nice to meet you. I was like, OK, I didn't ask her to engage I said nice to meet you and walked off. I knew who our ass was all over social media and shit with Michael, but anyways I was like, cool, so why is this man sweating and fucking me? Then I guess she went back and told him I ran into her some shit. He's been blowing up my phone all night. I knew my special night with Malachi was tonight, so I put him on DND. Remember when I excused myself from the table?"

"Yes!"

"He was texting me like, Kai, I know she approached you with lies, etc.

It's not true, baby. Let me explain blah blah blah,"

"But Kai. How did he know you were there with us?"

"Oh yeah, so I'm pulling out of my garage with Malachi. He pulled in and saw us. I guess I seen him, but I wasn't gonna let him fuck shit up for me, but he still managed to, huh. He followed us. I guess Michael texted me and told me if he didn't hear from me soon, he was gonna pull up. I was like fuck him. I didn't think he would... at a restaurant... at an establishment. My home, yes, but not a restaurant and cause a scene, fuck! I was wrong."

"It's OK, sis."

"Kassidy, no, it's not. I love Malachi. I could see the hurt in his eyes. He was asking me to marry him in front of everyone. Got my girls; y'all together, a great evening. Here comes this man with all his drama and bullshit. Spilling unnecessary information. Ridiculous. I just need to explain and let Malachi know. I chose him and him only. Kassidy, did I fuck up?"

She was hesitant, and I yelled. She told me to calm down. "Sorry, I'm just so frustrated."

We pulled up at the house. It was Michael Washington standing outside with his Range Rover.

"What are you gonna do?" "Nothing"

"I'm not in the mood for more bullshit tonight, right?" Kassidy said, "Just pull in your visitor spot." "Keshawn is behind you, right?"

"Yes."

"OK, girl! This is just too much for tea time." I chuckled. "Thanks, you're not helping."

I was getting out of the car. Here comes Michael. he said, "Baby…" "Just stop, Michael, I don't want this. It's been enough drama tonight!" He's like, "Let me explain!"

"What's to explain? I don't care, what the fuck don't you understand? I just don't give a fuck."

"Michael, just leave her alone…" Keshawn screams from the car.

He yells back, "Y'all need to mind your own fucking business. This has nothing to do with y'all because this is my situation. I need to fix it."

I interrupted, "There ain't shit to fix.."

"My baby. Listen, that woman lied. We are not engaged. She's not my fiancé…"

"Michael, stop it!"

"No, listen, that was my past, and she just doesn't get it."

"Michael, so she just knows you're in Tallahassee on GP?" I couldn't do this right then.

As tears were falling from my eyes, I couldn't even see at this point.

He yells out, "I love you KaiAndra. I came back for you to be my wife."

My girls are like, "What the fuck, at this moment and time, at the same time!!" I chuckled.

"Michael, stop this bullshit."

"No, I mean it. She got in my hotel, and the ring she was wearing is yours. I remember the ring you picked out four years ago. I was waiting for the right time to propose my love to you, baby. This isn't how I wanted it to happen..."

"Michael, please just go home or to your hotel. I can't do this right now." "KaiAndra!"

"NO! Not on your time. You did enough tonight; leave!" "Yeah Negro!" Kassidy and Keshawn yelled out at him.

"OK, baby, I will, but this isn't the last night or time that I'm coming over here."

"Whatever," I started walking away.

He yells out, "Mrs. Washington. I love you. That's my goal. Good night for now..." I just kept walking away.

What the fuck just happened... two men asking me to marry them on the same night on the same day. This isn't the way God! This isn't what I prayed for. Now, I need clarity and understanding.

I finally went to my condo, face sweating, hair a mess, makeup ran with Rancon eyes lashes, still on fire, though. I laughed out loud. My girls plopped on the couch.

Kassidy said, "Bestie, I know tonight was a lot. Just take time to adjust your crown and we all can get some rest and figure out this crazy stuff in the morning. We're gonna crash on the couch and in the guestroom."

"Thanks, y'all. I love y'all…" "We love you too, Sissy,"

I was walking towards my room and I heard a knock at my door. All I could think was, damn! Doesn't this man ever stop or give up?

Kassidy said, "You want me to grab the door?"

I said, "No, sissy, I will. This man has got to be stopped. I reached the door to open it and was about to scream, but I was shocked.

I was shocked when I saw and who I saw, it was him… Malachi! Oh my God! I can tell he's been crying. It's been raining. He's wet, his bald head still shining, and shit, he picks me up and hugs me as I wipe his head off. I look him in his eyes, and I kiss him passionately in front of my girls. I didn't care. I gave zero fucks at that moment. He puts me down and tells me he's sorry for leaving the restaurant. He's not weak. He just had a weak moment.

"Babe. Shush."

He told me, "Babe, today was a lot to break a man and leave the situation, but I know what we have and what we want, how I know what I want."

"No issue, baby. I know I want you to be my forever, always and forever," as tears were falling from my face. He has one or two as well. I wiped him and said, "Yes baby, I promise to love you every day and forever."

Keshawn said, "Yes! Congrats to you both.

Kassidy said, "OK sissy congrats! Do you want us to leave since your fiancé is here?"

I love my girls. I said, "If y'all OK to drive… if not, please stay…"

Kassidy said, "Bitch, I'm from the bricks. I'm good at driving." I laughed out loud.

Keshawn said, "Sissy. I'm good too. I got some dick looking for me too." I shook my head.

I said, "OK, y'all text me when y'all make it to your destinations." "Yes ma'am!" They gathered their purses and left.

He came over and picked me up and said, "I'm so lucky and happy you accepted to be Mrs. Combs. I love you, baby!"

"I love you too. Can I take you back to your room, baby?"

"You can take me wherever as long as I'm with you," I laugh out loud.

He placed me down and unzipped my beautiful dress and grabbed the hanger and placed it on my door. He kissed my shoulders and the back of my neck. He slid my strapless bra off. Babe has skills, too. I laughed out loud. He takes his tongue from the back of my neck to my red lace panties. He takes my red lace panties off with his teeth. Oh my God! This man gives me soft kisses on my ass. My red lace panties hit the floor. At this point, my nipples were hard as fuck, and pussy was so wet and juicy. I felt a smack on my ass. I turned around, and I kissed him. I unbuttoned his shirt and kissed his chest down to his pants, and I unbuttoned those.

I could tell he was ready for me, so I pushed him onto my bed as I took off his pants and boxer briefs. Oh well, my favorite when he wears those. I love him and crawled up to his dick and kissed it with soft kisses as I heard him say fuck I knew I was doing my job. I took all of his 8.5 inches and sucked from the tip to his shaft with enthusiasm, and my tongue gave him the stroke of pleasure.

He yelled out, "Mrs combs. Please come bounce on me, baby. I want to feel you as I climb up on that mountain."

I looked him in the eyes and told him, "I'm sorry for tonight, baby!" He interrupted me with his lips, "I love you."

"I love you too,"

"That's all that matters." He said.

He flipped me over and kissed my pierced nipples. They were hard as fuck. Oh my God, he sucks them so selectively, damn! He makes me cum from just that. He pushed himself inside of me, and we both moaned together.

"Yes, baby fuck me. Cum with me, baby!"

I felt my body getting warmer. He was getting faster and faster. I know he was about to cum. We said, "Fuck!"

I pushed him over and grabbed his dick to suck him empty. He tried to run for me all the time. It definitely does something to him. How did I get so lucky? I guess God didn't forget my address. It was just getting processed to be delivered to the correct address.

We were lying in bed, and I just looked at my hand, and my two-karat diamond was just blinking with my nails. How did this man know what I wanted? He never seems to not amaze me. I know I love him, and he loves me.

"So, babe!" He asked me, "Yes, babe,"

"So... Michael? When are we going to have this discussion? "We can... just not right now, please, as long as we have it, Kai." "Yes, babe... we can in the morning."

"Yes baby, good night!" "Good night."

Chapter 13
MotorMouth Sundaze

That was the best sleep I had in a while. Oh my God, I woke up to a chocolate, fine-ass man in my bed. That's my man, my fiancé, my friend, my lover, and my soon-to-be husband. God is good all the time. He's still sleeping, and to just watch him sleep is so sexy. This man, my man, I didn't think I could love him or vice versa the way we fell in love with each other.

He wakes up, grabs me, and says, "Am I dreaming, or are you my soon-to-be wife?"

I pinched him. "Ouch," he yelps in pain.

"Well, guess you weren't dreaming." We both chuckle. "I guess I am," said Malachi.

"Yes, baby, I am so sorry about last night with Michael. I know you heard him say shit, and I know it hurt. I'm truly sorry from the bottom of my heart."

"Yes, baby, that shit was crazy last night, and yes, the jabs stung, but I just needed to clear my head and regroup because deep down, I know you love me."

"How? What made you finally believe me?"

"Honestly, you remember the morning I surprised you with flowers, breakfast, and morning dick, you showed me something. I've never seen one."

"What, babe?"

"You made time for me. No excuses, no bullshit." "Really?"

"Yes, Kai. The first year we fucked around, you were, 'No, I can't. Sorry, I can't.' Very seldom did we get to date. The months later into our year and you change, you let me in. Then, I fucked up with all my bullshit, and we kind of fell apart. I knew I needed to get my shit together,"

"And I'm proud of you for that, babe. Not just for me, but for you and your kids and us as a family."

"Oh my God, so did you tell your babies you wanted to marry me? I know they are a big part of your life."

"Absolutely, they helped me pick out your ring. My daughter loves you, Kai, despite her attitude." I roll my eyes.

"Yes, she's some work." We laughed out loud.

"But I love her too. I'm gonna get up and make us some breakfast. You like your usual: pancakes with crispy edges, fluffy scrambled eggs with cheese and pepper, turkey sausage, and your Cream Brulé coffee?"

"Oh my God, babe, you do know your lady. Yes, to all of it, Malachi.

Yes, baby, I love you so much." "I love you too, wife."

"I like the ring."

"Well, it's about noon, and my phone hasn't been ringing... Oh my God, because it's still on DND," shaking my head. Lord, my girls have been calling, texting, FaceTiming. Michael called, texted, don't care. Wow, and who is this 655-999-9899 number several times? That's alarming. What the fuck now, who the fuck now? Let me call my girl back on FaceTime.

"Hey, Jefa, good morning, afternoon." "Hey, girl," "Hey, how are you?"

"Much better," they say. "We see y'all glowing and shit."

"Yes, Malachi is my person, y'all. I love him so much, Kassidy." "Oh, that's so great, Kai."

Keshawn blurts out, "So, bitch, what are you gonna do about Michael Washington and his proposal?"

"Keshawn, really? Seriously, I can't just have a moment of happiness for 24 hours."

"Oops, sorry."

"You haven't told Malachi?"

"No, only half of it, but he knows now. Thanks." Click. I hung the fucking phone up quick.

"Kai, what the fuck did Keshawn say?"

"Calm down, babe. I haven't had a chance to talk or tell you this." "Well, now is a good fucking time, don't you think?"

"Baby, please calm down, Malachi."

"Well, when did you think it was a good time? The man came into the restaurant, acted a fool, and ruined an amazing evening, so no time like the present."

"Okay, babe, calm down," "Kandra. I'm listening," "Sweetheart. Please relax." "Okay, I guess, after we left..." "Skip the bullshit, babe." "Well, damn,"

"I don't care, get to the point. So what, this fool asked you to marry him?"

"Okay, he was in the garage, babe, when we got here. And when I got out of the car with the girls, he was asking to talk, I said no, go home, Michael. And he kept on as I was walking away. He yelled out some shit.

And said things weren't true. He loves me. That's why he asked me to be his wife."

"Oh, so you had no idea about this man wanting you to be his wife?" "No, baby, I promise."

"So, what the fuck did you say?"

"I told him to go home, and I went to the condo and was talking to the girls. That's when I tried calling you, babe, I promise. That's it, this new girl, something else."

"'Kandra, there's something else about him that I just don't trust. This is something you haven't told me."

"Yes, baby, you're right. Can we talk about this after breakfast, please?"

Malachi says, "I've lost my appetite. I'm going to shower and go home to change clothes, and we can discuss this bullshit tonight. I'll be back to my lady later."

I stopped him before he could leave the kitchen. I took his face, looked him in his eyes, and told him,

"When we have disagreements or arguments, I will let you have your space, but I will not go to bed upset, mad, or angry. I love you, babe."

Yes, we did do some things, and he kissed me on the forehead and said, "I understand, and we can talk later about it."

I didn't let go. I kissed him several times.

"Malachi, baby, I choose you. I am choosing a life with you. I love you.

You're my heart. You have my heart. My heart is with you."

"I know. I love you. I'm just beyond frustrated how this man is disrespectful and the shit he's doing,"

"Malachi. I will handle it, I promise. On Monday morning, he questions, "Why the fuck Monday and not now, babe?"

"I told you it's more, and you want to leave and talk later, remember?"

He replied, "Let me shower. Matter of fact, let's shower, and let me taste you so I can calm down."

We laughed out loud.

"So tasting me is gonna help you calm down?" I started blushing. "Okay, babe, who the hell was gonna turn down some firehead from

your man?"

I was just in the damn dog house because my Bestie talks too much. Woof! What a fucking morning, afternoon, whatever. But my breakfast is fresh and looks delicious.

"Babe. Let me warm it up and feed you, babe. Bring your fine ass and get in the shower."

"Coming," he says.

I took a sip of my coffee. Shit, it was good, hot too. This man, my man, my fiancé, he can cook, he can fuck, suck, and shop. Damn, he's a provider, lover, and loyal. The consistency is so amazing. I've been praying for that for us. I am in love.

'Who skips threw their house? Ha ha, me,' I thought as I removed my robe. Of course, I'm naked under, my nipples hard as bricks. His dick was just staring at me in the shower. Woo, he has such a pretty dick. It's gorgeous. Can't say a lot of men have pretty dicks, shit.

"Ooh, babe, the water is amazing."

He starts washing my body, my back, and my arms. He turns around, kisses me so passionately, pulls me away, and washes my breasts, my stomach, and then my thighs. He takes my loofah and washes my privates as I moan like I'm ready to fuck. He teases me, rinses me off, and selectively sucks my pierced nipples. I'm moaning. He's moaning.

"Babe," I call out.

"Shush," he said as he slowly pushed me down on the nook in my shower.

He pushes up my legs and opens them as he passionately kisses my lips and teases them. Oh my God, this man is going to make me have an orgasm and come, along with screaming shit. Wow, as I'm moaning, grabbing my breast softly with one hand and his bald head with the other, he's getting more aroused.

"I feel I am about to come," he stops, just turns around, and pulls me close to him.

He guides himself into me, and I let out soft screams. "Yes, Malachi, fuck me. This is your pussy forever, baby," I reassure him.

"Are you sure this is what you want forever, Kai?" he asks. "Yes, baby, I want us every day forever."

Oh my God, this man was showing me why I have been sprung for two years.

"Yes, Malachi, yes baby, fuck me."

I know we are both about to cum, I came first, but he hasn't. I know it's close; he's getting faster so I pull away and turn and sit on the nook and finish my man off for breakfast.

I bounced on that beautiful chocolate dick until he came. I couldn't get up; I came again, shit. Our sex is so powerful and amazing. How could a lady ever complain? Plus, my man is fire, too. We stayed in the shower a few more minutes as I cleaned him up. He looked me in my eyes, and he had a tear fall.

"'Baby, I've been praying for this moment. I got myself together, and you didn't wander off while I was getting myself together. I love you, and I will make sure we are always good as long as there is breath in my body." Oh my God, this man.

"Okay, babe, let's do this thing called marriage together."

My Sunday went amazing, but I knew what came next Monday… Michael. This man wasn't going to stop at nothing, but I knew I had to before shit got dangerous. What the fuck was I gonna say to where it couldn't hurt him or wouldn't hurt him?

What am I saying? This man tried to destroy me at dinner last night. I just had to be real and let shit go. This was gonna be crazy. What was going to happen with the investment? The investors will pull the deal. Fuck, this was a great opportunity to put my business on the map. Shit, but I love my man more at this point.

Michael's got groupies and shit, yeah, and someone breaking into his hotel room? Get the fuck out of here, and someone stealing my ring that he knows? Please, bullshit. Oh well, we'll see you tomorrow. I can't worry.

Today has been so good. Let me get fed by my man and enjoy the rest of our day. Football later, the Rams and Greenbay play today, and my honey is staying the night. Yes, can I say winning? I guess he will talk later. Pussy is a strong tool. Laugh out loud.

Chapter 14
Truthful Monday

Welp, my annoying alarm went off, and Malachi left early this morning to get his day started. He left me with him on my lips. I love that this man chose an outfit for me and laid it out, so let me get dressed. I text Michael to meet me at my office at 10 AM. Nobody will be there until after one today, so it's just us. I pray this all goes well, shaking my head. I'm nervous as hell because I don't know how he's going to react. Should I talk about my investors first or the fact that I'm getting married and accepted Malachi's proposal? Oh well, so I called Michael.

"Hello, beautiful."

"Yeah, yeah, blah blah blah blah blah blah. Meet me at my office at 10 AM."

"Your office, not your house?"

"I need to talk, Michael. My office," and I hung up.

Who does he think he is? This man is nuts. Time was flying, and I had so much to do. I had butterflies thinking about my man, my honey, my future husband, my fiancé. Oh my God, I'm really engaged. Is this what I prayed for, my own Cinderella moment? It's my turn, my time, Miss Keandra McCombs. Oh my God, I just love how it sounds. Looking at my fabulous, gorgeous bling ring, oh, and my nails set it off.

My ass was in her daydream and smiling and stuff. My secretary, Miss Barnes, Mr. Washington, is here to see you. My heart just sank into my stomach. Fuck, I don't know why discombobulated, "Go ahead and send them in. Thank you," woo. OK, girl, you got this. You are in love with Malachi. Stay strong.

He walks into my office, sharp as attack, cream soup, blazer, jacket, jeans, white button-down, fresh shave, smelling good as hell. Snap out of it. He's not your future husband.

"Hello, Mr. Washington." "Miss Barnes, touché."

"Please have a seat. I just got comfortable." "Oh, so you're comfortable," he states. "You know what I mean, Michael."

"Well," he starts with, "Keandra, let me start by saying my apologies about Saturday. I was way out of control and out of line and have never acted that way, but no," he says, "let me finish."

"Yes, all right, I guess. Go ahead," I say.

"To see another man have you drives me insane. It drives me crazy. I don't like it. It puts me in my feelings. Now, for Kimberly, Michael, hold on, let me explain."

"Michael, I don't care." "Really?"

"Yes, really, it's water under the bridge."

He's looking at me crazy. "Don't look at me like that. Listen, I had time to think," he says.

"Me too, but I asked, let me go first," he's like, "Ladies first."

"Michael, you had my heart for five years and some. I gave you my heart, my love, my soul. We were inseparable, unstoppable, but you broke us with your dreams, not our dreams, which I am very proud of you for. I cannot forget the heartbreak, that empty feeling. With that being said, I moved on. I found somebody, and I found someone. No, I should say someone found me. It was so cute in the beginning, leaving heart emojis on my window for months at our Thirsty Thursday spot. Anyways, he took the time to get to know me and still is."

I hear a big sigh. Then, here it comes.

"So, you made your decision because you're wearing his ring. I have, so your dick fling is now on your way to being your husband now. Come on, you're kidding, right?"

"See, Michael, you see it as a dick fling. I see it as a man I fell in love with over time."

He's upset at this point. "So fuck, what I gotta say, what can I say, right?

Fuck what I've done to put us here?" "What do you mean, Michael?"

"You just showed up, and you didn't contact me, nothing." "How the fuck could I? You had me blocked for fucking years!"

"So what, Michael? There were other ways. You showed up at my damn house for crying out loud at 11:15 PM one night."

"So you're saying you don't love me, KaiAndra?"

"Michael, I love you, yes, but I'm not in love with you. That's a big part of it, Kai. I've done so much building for you and to get that courage. I finally showed up because I didn't know you would reject me the way you are doing right now."

"What did you build?" "I built my own shit."

"Oh, you think that, huh?"

"What the fuck are you talking about?"

"So you think your investments are all from you?" "Well, yes, except for the two the other day."

"Nope, so half of your investors are from me, sweetheart. I've invested millions to see your business grow because I felt like I owed you from how you grooved mine up and got it started. So I felt I needed to do the same and return the favor."

"Well, thank you. I really appreciate that, Michael. I never knew you were a silent partner or investor. Well, with that being said, why come out and tell me now?"

"Because I want you to be my wife. I have plans for us, Kai, and I've already sold two of my businesses to move here to Tallahassee, Florida, and grow my life with you. I've purchased the house, our house, a six-bedroom, three-bath home with a patio view off the master bedroom. Just what you asked for. It might've been years ago, but I never forgot. The big backyard, what you always wanted for the kids we are supposed to have together."

Oh my God, this man. What the fuck? I am blown away. This man's voice was cracking, and shit like he was about to cry.

"I hear you, Michael, but why? You didn't call me, write to me, or something. Why would you do all this without researching my life? You called me private the other night, so I'm confused by all of this."

Woman. I love you, and I know I fucked up, Kai. I did my research. Our mutual friends said you were still single not seeing anyone. That's because I have kept my love life private since the last relationship with you."

"Nobody knows shit. Nobody knows nothing about my love life but myself, my girls, and Malachi. So what now? You gonna pull my investors and shit? In my head, I'm like fuck, what if he does some bullshit? My business has just started taking off. My business is in the top three in the East Coast and upcoming in the West."

"I'm not sure what you mean, Kai."

"Negro, yes the fuck you do. Don't play with me."

"So you think I'm that fucked up to think I would pull my investors and lose my money too?"

"Damn, this really fucks me up. You think of me this way. You know what, Kai, let me go and get the fuck out of here until I gather my thoughts and my feelings. I am clearly hurt by this now. You know what, Kai? Let me go and get the fuck out of here until I gather my thoughts and my feelings. I am clearly hurt at this present time."

"Hurt? Are you fucking serious? You're hurt? Get the fuck out. You left me, Michael. You vanished over money."

"Fuck me. Remember that shit all over social media, 'What a bitch.' Ha ha, and smiling and shit, then come home and expect me not to be waiting on your light-bright ass four years later. You trippin', then you get coffee and approach me talking about, 'I hope you are coming to our nuptials."

"Yeah, fuck you. I tried to explain, Kandra."

"Explain what? The bitch you were fucking or still fucking is delusional and shit. Hell no. The grass ain't always greener. Money might never run out for you. My love does come to an end," I yell at him.

He asks, "What the fuck does that mean?"

"It means love dies. You don't mean that shit to her." "The hell I do-"

"Bye Michael"

"I love you to death, and that man you think you're gonna marry, ain't it, Kai."

"Oh yeah? Why do you think you know so much?"

"You can look at him. He doesn't know how to love. He looks like he's just winging it with you."

How the fuck does he know this? This man knows this shit for real because I felt like that in the beginning with Malachi too. He's partly right, honestly, but I'll never come out and admit it.

"Whatever, Michael."

"Kai, please think about it. This isn't over for us. I know you love me.

The passion, the chemistry, and the drive we have are real." He comes over to me. "Michael, I'm not in the mood."

As he wraps those big muscles around me and hugs me, he whispers in my ear. "This is my pussy, and your heart belongs to me, Kandra. I will take care of you and give you the world."

He looks me in my face and says, "You're mine," and kisses me.

I was hesitant, and he kept kissing me. I engaged back and kissed him back and said, "Please leave," he replied, "For now, I will. But I'll keep coming back until I have you forever. And oh, let me know if you want to see the house I bought for you and the investors. Need your answer today by 3 PM central mountain time. Have an amazing day, babe," and shut my door.

Oh my God, why? Why? Why? Fuck this drama? Why? How's this happening to me? Shit, Cinderella, Snow White, Princess Jasmine didn't have all this kind of drama. This man bought me a house, what the fuck? Oh my God, my dream house at that. What in the entire fuck, this man, shit. Malachi, my man, my husband-to-be, probably ain't even thought that far, like I own my condo, and he owns his house, and I love his house. I was gonna ask about that. I have some decisions to make. Gotta put on my big girl panties and tell my man what the fuck is going on before I lose him. I don't wanna lose him.

Will I lose him? Will he trust me? Shit? I've worked hard for both things, my business and my man. Ugh, God, it's me again, KaiAndra. I need you. Order my steps. I have some serious thinking to do.

Chapter 15
Discussions & Decisions

Damn, where did the time go? It was 2 PM and I had to make a decision in an hour for my investors, but I needed to call Malachi and tell him everything that had been going on and what I just found out before I did that, huh? Shit, here goes nothing. The phone is ringing and ringing and ringing, and he finally answers.

"Hey, baby," he says, "you must be busy."

"Yeah, it's been crazy as hell in here today in my office," "Really? I thought nobody would get there till about 1 o'clock."

"Yeah, but I had some discussions I needed to have happen before then, what's up? You okay? What's going on?"

"What I had to talk to you about was Michael- "Keandra, what the fuck he do now?"

"Babe, calm down. This was before Saturday."

"What the fuck do you mean? What was before Saturday? Okay, well, I'm listening."

Here we go, God, this man! Don't let me lose it. Don't let him lose it.

Don't let me lose him. I love this man.

"So, remember when I told you I had investors come up from different states on the West Coast to learn more about my company?"

"Yes, baby,"

"Well, it was Michael and his investors." "What? What the fuck are you saying to me," "calm down," "since when?

"Since always, I've never told you because we never got a chance to talk Saturday night, so hold on, babe, there's more,"

"Seriously?"

"yes, so he's been funding my business for years, and I never knew it." "Keandra, really, you didn't know he was funding your businesses?" "No, babe, I didn't, babe. I'm sorry, I didn't know."

"So, you expect me to believe this shit, babe?" "I promise I didn't know."

"So, what else, Kai?" "Babe, please," "what else?"

"He sold two of his companies and bought into a business here for takeover, and he is moving back here."

"You're fucking kidding me right now, right?"

"No, babe, I'm sorry. I love you, and I never knew any of this. This is unreal, babe. I'm sorry, sweetie."

"How would you feel if my ex came and sought into my business and moved here?"

"I understand that now."

"You don't. You can't possibly understand let me make it more real for you. Let me add oh, and I fucked her too."

"Come on, that's not fair. We said no strings,"

"but you knew I was trying to get serious with you again,"

I can hear this conversation going left, "Okay, Malachi, well, here it goes, the last piece... he bought me a house."

"What? So, let me guess, he wants to steal, marry you, and be his wife."

Crickets, I don't say anything. He says, "Hello?" I didn't want to answer this, "Oh, now you're quiet,"

"Babe."

"No, answer the fucking question, yes or no?" "Babe."

"No, fuck that, I love you."

"No answer, huh," sigh, "yes, Kai, I'm not going to compete with this man,"

"Babe-"

"Let me finish, it's obvious y'all have history, and I don't want to get hurt because you don't know what the fuck you want,"

"That's not true. If that's the case, why have you hid this from me until now?"

"Because I just found out today."

"Oh, you expect me to believe that shit, so you seen him," "Yes."

"Wow, another office visit."

"Yes, I asked him to come here so we can talk." "Wow, did you fuck him?"

"Excuse me?"

"Don't play with me, Keoandea. Did you fuck him?"

"No. You really think after I accepted your ring, I would do something like that and hurt you, Michael? I mean, Malachi."

"Wow, so you calling me that, Negro, now, get the fuck out of here, you know what, I gotta go do what the fuck I want, you do you, it will determine what happens with us,"

"What does that mean,"

"Just what the fuck I said. I love you, KaiAndra, but I'm not gonna beg or stand around why you figure out what man you want,"

"Babe, no,"

"You need to figure it out."

So what will happen if I accept this offer? Will he say fuck it and call off our engagement? I'm really scared to ask, oh my God, why, Lord?

"Malachi?" "Yes"

"Babe, sorry, are you saying if I take this offer with the investors, you don't wanna marry me, babe?"

"Imma let you make that decision. That's not for me to make, just know everything you decide has consequences, so I'm not seeing you tonight."

"Malachi, babe, I will be there if that's what you want," "Hell yes, it is, but what, Kai, I want my business too,"

"Babe-" click, did this man really hang up on me, "hello, hello," oh my God, he did, now he pissed me off, I called him back, but voicemail, so I called again, voicemail, is this man for real, he better hope like hell, his phone died, I picked up the work phone, voicemail.

OK, well, fuck, my man is upset. I understand, but damn, it's 2:45 central mountain time. I gotta make a final decision, fuck, fuck, fuck, fuck, here goes nothing. I called into our Zoom call.

"Everyone, it's KaiAndra Barnes. How's everyone doing today?" "Hey, Cassandra, we are all wonderful."

"Well, that's great news. I didn't want to keep y'all long and let y'all know I've made a decision, and I'm going to accept the offer y'all have extended and can't wait to start working with you all on the plans for the West Coast office. Of course, Michael's on the Zoom call."

"Congratulations. We are excited you decided to collaborate with us, and we look forward to a successful business adventure."

I'm thinking, of course, you are, Negro, I was fucking you. "Hello, KaiAndra. Are you still there?"

"Yes, sorry. Thank you for this opportunity, and I will see y'all soon.

Have a great night," I quickly disconnected the call.

Oh my God, what did I just do? I accepted these investors, and my man is not gonna be happy about it.

Well, will he leave me? Will Malachi understand? Will he love me through all this bullshit? Oh shit, shit, shit, I need to put it on him hard tonight so he can realize I love his ass. Pussy can help a little bit. Laugh out loud, chuckle. Let's hope tonight can... I tried him again, still voicemail, shaking my head. OK, Malachi... I love me some of him and that dick too.

Woo, what the fuck shall I do? What am I gonna do? Will Malachi still love me working with my ex? Will I lose my man if I choose my business? I want them both. Will Michael say fuck me and destroy my dream because I haven't chosen him? Will he never let me go? These decisions are life-changing or will they be?

About the Author

My name is Kamrin Cambric I am originally from Los Angeles, CA but currently live in the Midwest. When I'm not slaying nails and bracelets, I'm sipping margaritas writing and sharing some good laughs. I love to mingle with different people, I am a social butterfly and love to inquire about certain things and individuals. I have been writing for years but never thought I would be writing books, , until this moment. I lost a very important lady in my life, my mother, we shared all kind of stories laughs tears etc. I would tell her my deepest darkest juicy stories. So because shes in heaven, I took my writing to a whole other level. I love passion affection and fairytale stories, so I use my imagination on many life situations between friends, husbands, wives, girlfriend/boyfriends etc and just write and make them feel real. I love juicy passion and suspense reads, so I just put my spin on them. I hope you all enjoy because I have that passion to fulfill your eyes. I am a sucker for love romance suspense and can be timid with a touch of heartbreak but a suspenseful ending. Ive been in healthcare all my life so know its time to follow my dreams.

www.ingramcontent.com/pod-product-compliance
Lightning Source LLC
LaVergne TN
LVHW010558070526
838199LV00063BA/5009